THE PEACEKEEPER

by Ray Hogan

The townspeople of Moriah had come to Luke Brazil for help. A group of wild cow hands were tearing the town apart. Would he accept the job of marshal? Luke thought he had put his past behind him. A former lawman and bounty hunter, Luke now owned a ranch and wanted only to settle down with Jenny Lockwood. But when they told him Jenny was trapped in the local hotel, he knew what his decision had to be. So he strapped on his Colt .45 and pinned on the marshal's star. One man alone, he went out to put an end to the violence.

THE
PEACE KEEPER

Also Available in Large Print
by Ray Hogan

The Yesterday Rider

THE
PEACE KEEPER

Ray Hogan

G.K.HALL&CO.
Boston, Massachusetts
1979

Library of Congress Cataloging in Publication Data

Hogan, Ray 1908-
  The peace keeper.

  Large print ed.
  1. Large type books. I. Title.
[PZ4.H716Pe 1978b] [PS3558.03473]   813'.5'4
ISBN 0-8161-6660-9   78-27163

28237

Published in Large Print by arrangement with Doubleday & Company, Inc.

Set in Compugraphic 18 pt English Times

to
Delia McKnight Clayton
. . . who now walks with the angels

1

"The marshal's dead. Was one of them Texas trail hands. A stray bullet, we figure."

Luke Brazil, standing in the doorway of his two-room shack, considered John Ashford's words with no change of expression. It was late in the afternoon of a June day and the heat in the confines of the small structure was oppressive.

"So?"

Ashford, owner of Moriah's principal general store and mayor of the settlement, glanced uncertainly at the two men who had accompanied him on the mission: the Reverend Myron Kilburn, pastor of Moriah's only church, and Aaron Horn, one of the merchants.

"We — we're asking for your help. Like for you to pin on Hurley's star, take over

1

the job as marshal until we can find somebody to replace him."

From a back corner of the room a short, derisive laugh sounded. Brazil did not trouble to look around at the elderly man slouching in one of the two crudely built, cowhide chairs placed against the wall. Arkansas — Arky — was an old friend who had been with him for years. They'd met by accident. He'd found Arky cornered in a border-town saloon one night with the odds all wrong, had stepped in and bailed him out. Arky's gratitude had never diminished. "Seems things've changed some," he said dryly. "Got us a horse of a different color."

Luke's wide shoulders stirred indifferently. "Ought to be somebody else around —"

"But not with your experience," Ashford said hurriedly. "We figure you once being a lawman and a bou —"

Brazil's set lips cracked into a humorless smile at the mayor's hesitancy. "Go ahead, say it: bounty hunter."

"Bounty hunter," Ashford finished lamely. "We don't mean no disrespect,

Brazil. We'd like for you to understand that, and if the townspeople have been sort of, well, unfriendly and standoffish in the past it's all because they never got to know you."

"But now they've gone and got themselves a catamount by the tail and they're right anxious to get real friendly," Arkansas observed sarcastically, rising and moving toward the door. "Luke, you're plain loco if you go chancing your hide for them —"

Brazil raised a broad hand, motioned the older man to silence. He reckoned what Arky said was true; it had taken a long time and a lot of hard work to get where he was — the owner of a small ranch — and there was still a long way to go before he reached the point where he felt he could consider himself a successful rancher.

He had always wanted a place of his own where he could raise cattle for the market and do a little horse breeding on the side. It had been an ambition of his from the start and he'd set it as his life's goal — one to be reached as soon as possible. He'd taken several jobs, finally settling down as a lawman in the Texas Panhandle country because the wages were regular and he could do a bit of planning.

But the money was small and the capital he felt necessary accumulated slowly. Eventually he handed in his badge and turned bounty hunter. He spent five years of his life at that danger-ridden profession, tracking down and cashing in on wanted outlaws, but the day did come at last when he had enough cash to purchase the small spread he had lined up and stock it with a few steers.

Now, two years later, he had a growing herd of five hundred head and was thinking about building a regular ranch house with all the trimmings — one he'd be proud to offer the girl he felt would consent to be his wife. . . . Arky was right; he'd be a damned fool to risk throwing it all away for a town full of people — except for a few — that had shunned him because of his past.

Brazil shook his head. "Peace keeping's not in my line — not any more."

Aaron Horn, a graying, intense man, took a step forward. "I don't think you realize how bad things are!" he said, his lined face taut with worry. "Them Texans are fair taking the town apart!"

Luke smiled. Folks were inclined to term all trail hands who pushed herds to the shipping points "Texans" whether they were from the Lone Star State or not. "The town's been a railhead for cattle several years," Brazil said. "Expect this's not the first time a bunch of drovers've taken over the place — or tried to."

"No, but, always before, they've stayed pretty well on the other side of the dead line — in Perdition. They're paying no mind to that rule now, and with Jesse Hurley dead there ain't nobody can control them."

"We are desperate," Kilburn, a tall, somber man said in his deep, echoing voice. "I appeal to you, sir. There are women and children in danger. And with night coming on —"

"Can't some of you get together and do something about it?" Arkansas cut in angrily. "Reckon there's a plenty of you that knows how to pull the trigger on a gun. And if there ain't, now sure would be a fine time for learning.''

Ashford stirred wearily. Once a man of consequence in a large eastern city, he had been forced by ill health to sacrifice his holdings and move west.

"We talked about that," he said. "We agreed we would stand no chance against Sobel and his drovers."

"Sobel?" Luke repeated. "He the trail boss?"

The mayor nodded. "Parley Sobel. Owner of the herd, too. Soon as they got the cattle in the pens, he turned his hired hands loose. They've been running wild through the town ever since. I've never seen things so bad — not in all the years I've been in Moriah. I don't know what's come over those men."

"I reckon there's a price on prosperity, after all," Arkansas murmured, stroking his beard.

Moriah had never been one of the major locations for shipping cattle to eastern markets, handling perhaps no more than thirty or forty thousand head in a season. It was, however, a convenient one for ranchers in certain areas of Texas,

6

Colorado, and New Mexico and its western half, now the Territory of Arizona, since being so designated during the war.

But it was becoming better known, and its popularity was increasing, as it permitted the drovers to cut off as much as two weeks from a drive that would otherwise be compelled to continue on to Trinity Crossing, the next railhead. Undoubtedly there would be more and more herds driven in as the word spread, and Moriah could look forward to being one of the principal shipping points.

"For certain," Horn said. "And folks've been grumbling right along about how them trail hands act. Some are saying the extra business ain't worth all the damage that's done. Talk's going to get louder now, what with the marshal getting killed."

"Was accidental," Ashford reminded the clothing-store merchant.

"Accident or not, Jesse's dead, and it wouldn't have happened if them hellhounds hadn't been running up and down the street shooting off their pistols and raising hob!"

"And they wouldn't be getting away with it if Hurley was alive and keeping them in Perdition!"

Horn snorted. "They wasn't across the line when one of them fired that stray bullet — if it was a stray. I don't figure they was paying any mind to him. They just took it in their heads to cross over the dead line and start hoorawing the town. They know dang well they ain't supposed to do that, but they went right ahead and done it anyway. If you'd —"

"Gentlemen," the Reverend Kilburn broke in gently, "this is getting us nowhere. While we're standing here blaming others, those hoodlums are terrorizing the town. If we can't persuade Mr. Brazil to help us, then we'd best try to think of something else."

"Like what?" Horn demanded, scrubbing at the sweat on his face. "It'd take the sheriff until morning to get here — even if we was lucky enough to catch him in his office at the county seat. And we sure can't figure on the Army."

Luke felt the eyes of John Ashford and the Reverend Kilburn pressing him, awaiting an answer of some sort — hoping for one of assent. But strapping on his gun was the last thing he wanted to do. When he'd hung it up after moving onto his ranch and turning his attention to raising beef, he hoped he was putting the weapon and his expertise with it behind him, and that he never again would be called upon to use it.

While he was unashamed of the fact, he'd had his time with guns and bullets, first in the war and then later as a lawman and outlaw hunter. The big Colt .45 had served him well, and with it he had accomplished his life's purpose — although there was small doubt it had left its grim mark upon him.

But that was the past, and he had no wish to reopen it. The new life he'd dreamed of was even better than visualized. He'd learned to not always be wary of the shadows, that there were men who were honest and could be trusted, that reality was not always cloaked in bitterness. A fine future lay ahead for him: the ranch he'd always wanted, a home, a wife and family, success and prosperity — it was all there if things continued to go as they were.

His relationship with Jenny Lockwood, daughter of Ben Lockwood, the owner of the largest ranch in the area, had strengthened steadily to the point where he knew she would consent to marriage if he were to ask. Pride, however, would not permit him to go that far — just yet. He'd not bring a woman like Jenny, who, as Lockwood's daughter, had all she wished, into a two-room shack to live.

But he was in the process of correcting that lack. He had plans to sell off a few head of stock and begin the construction of a new house before the summer was over. When that was done he would have something to offer Jenny Lockwood.

"We've just got to do something!" Luke heard Aaron Horn say in an exhausted sort of tone. "I got three daughters to worry about. They ain't safe — not nowhere in town — with them drunks running loose. And there's my store. They already busted one of my windows and helped themselves to a couple of hats I was displaying."

"Your store's not the only one that's suffered. There've been several broken into."

Horn swiped at the shine on his face. "Ain't claiming it is. Most everybody's getting hurt — but there ain't everybody with a family of girls like I got — and I'll tell you something, Brazil," the merchant added, pointing a stiff finger at Luke, "you best do a little worrying along that line, too."

Brazil's lank shape slowly drew to attention, and a hardness came into his pale eyes. Raising a hand, he ran fingers through his dark hair while a mixture of suspicion and alarm tightened his mouth.

"What are you getting at?"

"Just this," the merchant replied bluntly, "them drovers've got Jenny Lockwood and her ma penned up inside the hotel — afraid to come out."

Brazil's voice was cold, as insistent as winter's wind. "This true — or you saying it to get my help?"

It was John Ashford who answered. "The truth. They came in the morning to do some marketing and —"

"Where's Lockwood?"

"Out on the range somewhere, I suspect. Him and the boy both. I sent word to the ranch. Don't know whether it's reached Ben or not."

"I don't think Mrs. Lockwood and Jenny are in any great danger — leastwise long as they stay inside the hotel," Kilburn said, shaking his head. "Tom Carson has his doors closed and locked —"

"That won't mean nothing to them animals!" Aaron Horn shouted, once again wiping sweat from his strained features. "Jenny Lockwood is a mighty fine-looking young woman — if you don't mind my saying so, Brazil. And if a couple of them drunks get a look at her through the window, they're apt as not to kick in the door and grab her."

Ashford raised his hands in protest. "Now, Aaron, there's not much danger of that! Besides, Tom Carson'll look out for them."

Horn snorted. "Tom's getting on to seventy years old. He couldn't look out for hisself in a tight much less protect a woman from a couple of trail hands."

Brazil was paying no attention to the wrangling conversation. He had turned away, crossed the room, and under the disapproving eyes of Arkansas, he was taking his belt and gun from its peg on the wall.

"You're going to do it, I reckon," the older man said heavily.

Luke nodded as he swung the belt about his slim waist and tongued the buckle snugly. "No choice."

From near the doorway Aaron Horn murmured in relief. "Thank God," he said. "I — we can all breathe easier now. We're sure grateful to you."

"Saying that, Aaron speaks for all of us — for everybody in Moriah," Ashford said. "And your taking on the job, helping us, fills me with shame when I remember how the town — and I include myself — has treated you."

Brazil had taken a box of cartridges from a nearby shelf, was filling the empty loops in the belt. His shoulders moved indifferently.

"We wouldn't blame you none if you told us all to go to hell," John

13

Ashford continued.

Luke was going about his preparations hurriedly; it was clear that he felt the situation in the settlement was urgent. "I've got a thick hide," he said. "Being in the business I was in, it was necessary. . . . Be a good idea if you'd head on back to town. I want you to pass the word on that I'll be acting marshal. I don't want any misunderstandings with anybody."

Ashford said, "I'll take care of it. Anything else?"

"Keep everybody off the street — if you can."

"They're mostly off now," Horn said. "Folks are too scared to be out, what with horses pounding up and down and guns going off like firecrackers on Independence Day."

"We'll see to it," the mayor assured Brazil. "Now, if you've got a minute I'd best swear you in officially. I want anything you do to be legal."

Luke, the belt filled and settled about his waist, reached for his hat, nodded impatiently. "Go ahead."

14

Ashford raised his hand, quoted the brief, necessary oath, and when Brazil had signified his acceptance, took the star worn by the late Jesse Hurley and pinned it on Luke's shirt pocket.

"Makes it official," Ashford said, stepping back. "You can appoint yourself a deputy if you want one."

Brazil lifted the heavy Colt revolver from its holster, twirled the cylinder, and tested the hammer with his thumb. "Probably need one. . . ."

The Reverend Kilburn extended his hand. "I want to say good luck, Marshal," he said as Brazil dropped the pistol back into its oiled leather sheath. A wry smile split his thin lips. "I hope you can accomplish your task without that — without bloodshed."

Arkansas, sullenly quiet during the past few minutes, swore under his breath. "Preacher, that's like hoping you can stick your hand into the fire and not get yourself burned," he said in disgust.

"I realize that," Kilburn said wearily, "but it costs nothing to hope — and I have faith that one day soon guns will

15

no longer be the way we settle our problems.''

"I reckon that'll be a spell yet," Arkansas replied.

"It could start the day we quit letting trail hands come into our town!" Aaron Horn declared, and turned back through the doorway. "Come on, John, Reverend. I just got to get home. Them girls of mine — and my store —"

"Yes, we'd all better get back," Ashford said, hastening to catch up with the merchant and Kilburn. He paused, glanced over his shoulder to Brazil. "When —"

"Soon as I can saddle my horse and ride in," Luke said, anticipating the man's question. "Be in mighty few minutes."

Moriah's mayor bobbed, crossed to the waiting buggy, and crowded onto the seat with the two other men. As Horn cut the vehicle about and struck for the road, Arkansas stepped up into the doorway.

"They're sure friendly — when they're aneeding help. Still say you're a dang fool to be doing this."

"Maybe," Brazil said, starting for the

16

rear of the shack. "Got to get my horse."

Arkansas came about and began to follow. "I reckon it ain't so much the town and the fix it's got itself in as it is the lady you're aworrying about."

Luke halted in the small kitchen of the shack. He smiled faintly. Arkansas always referred to Jenny Lockwood as *the lady,* and usually with a certain amount of stiffness.

"You're right. . . ."

The old man nodded crisply. "Then, soon's you see to it that her and her ma are out of town, where they can't be bothered, you can turn over that star to them counterjumpers and get on back here where you belong — let them look after their own skins."

Brazil considered Arkansas narrowly. "You figure I'd do something like that?"

The older man shrugged. "Naw, sure not. I was just talking to hear myself rattle."

Luke continued to study his friend. "There more to this than that? You thinking maybe I can't hold my own against a bunch of trail hands — that

I've slowed up?"

Arky brushed at his beard. "Well, now that you've brought it to mind," he replied coolly, "it has been a time since you made your living drawing quick and shooting straight."

"There's been no change —"

"Expect that's right, but I figure it would be smart for me to trot along with you, sort of keep an eye on your hind side. You're going to be needing a deputy. Reckon I'm him."

Brazil gave that brief thought as he stepped out into the yard. He could think of no one he'd prefer to have siding him.

"I'm obliged to you," he said, "but I want you to stay here right now, get something together for the hands to eat. They'll be coming in for supper pretty soon."

Arkansas swore. "Hell, Earl and Chaplin are growed men. They can fend for themselves!"

"I know that, but there's some explaining that needs doing and it'll be up to you, because I've got to get to town quick as I can. Tell them I want them to look after things till I get back — or you do. I don't want the place going to hell while I'm gone. After you've told them what it's all about, and fed them, come on in. I'll be at the marshal's office. If I'm not, wait for me there."

"If you're half smart you'll stay there till I come," Arkansas said pointedly. "You ain't going to get no help from any of them counterjumpers — not when it comes down to shooting."

"Not expecting any," Brazil said, and hurried on to the corral.

2

Moriah lay in the swale that separated the Skull Mountains to the west from the vast plains that extended, seemingly limitlessly, eastward. Not a large settlement — a single main street and two dozen or so buildings, not counting those that made up Perdition, the saloon-and-bawdy-house area adjacent to the cattle pens and railroad spur — it existed solely for the convenience of the ranchers, a few homesteaders, and those who made use of the railhead.

In the beginning the spur was its sole function, but as the county slowly acquired residents in the form of cattle growers and small-acreage farmers, the thin scatter of huts began to increase in number; merchants appeared on the scene and opened stores; small, one-room saloons multiplied, enlarged to provide not only drink but women, dance, and gambling for trail-weary drovers most of whom had been in the saddle for weeks.

Thus, eventually Moriah was a firmly established town complete with mayor, lawman, business concerns of all sorts, a church, a school — and all the usual vices. When the latter became a problem, the citizenry designated the area northeast of the main business and residential district and set apart by Dead Ute Creek, which coursed down from the Skulls, as the red-light section.

The area across the watery dead line quickly became known as Perdition, and the arrangement worked fairly well although, admittedly, there were occasions when drovers, emboldened by the fiery, gut-chewing liquor served in the Horsehead and similar saloons on the yonder side of the creek, crossed over to have their moments of fun harassing the more staid and proper of Moriah. Such was ordinarily of short duration, as the town marshal, usually with the co-operation of the trail boss or the owner of the herd, quickly chased the noisy offenders back across the dead line. But that, too, saw change as more and more herds were driven in to take advantage of the railroad's most southwesterly located shipping point.

Tougher crews began to frequent the area. Drovers from as far south as deep Texas and Mexico gradually became as common as those from the ranches in New Mexico, upper Arizona, the Panhandle, and Colorado, and all too often, the drive finished and footloose, they stayed on, spending their time in Perdition until their money ran out, whereupon they either sought other means for financing themselves or, under threat of the law, moved on.

Luke Brazil realized that that was the source of the trouble in Moriah as he pushed his horse at steady gallop for the settlement. The town now had the riffraff, the trail scum, to reckon with — a by-product of its own growth. Arky had been right when he'd said there was a price on prosperity.

The sun had dropped behind the Skulls,

and a pale amber glow had spread across the cedar-studded slopes when Luke broke out onto the long flat that led into the town. Immediately, he heard the faint popping of pistol shots, and reckoned the drovers were still having their way.

Although a certain amount of anxiety filled his mind where Jenny Lockwood and her mother were concerned, he was not too worried about them. As long as they remained inside, off the street, they were in no great danger. From his experience with drivers, he knew they seldom forced themselves into a residence or a business building, but confined their activities to the streets and alleys, along, of course, with the saloons that countenanced their shenanigans.

But Luke Brazil was taking nothing for certain; there were always the exceptions — and there was the possibility that Jenny would make an attempt to depart — thus he had ridden hard to cover the twelve miles between his ranch and the settlement as fast as possible.

He came in behind McKenzie's Livery Stable, at the extreme southern end of the street, and swinging into the vacant lot that separated the broad, low-roofed structure from its neighbor, drew to a halt in the lengthening shadows to have his look.

Dust hung in the canyon-like area between the twin rows of buildings like a brown cloud. The smell of gunpowder was in the air, and the crack of pistols, shouts, and the thud of horses' hoofs were constant in the rising night.

There were at least a dozen riders racing back and forth along the street, firing at the signs merchants had erected in front of their establishments — always a favorite target — at tin cans, buckets, lanterns, and anything else that tempted a marksman's aim. Down in front of Rankin's Gun & Saddle Shop a fight was in progress: the two contestants, encouraged by the yells of half a dozen or more other trail hands, were swaying and surging as they grappled in a swirling boil of tan.

Perdition was not being neglected. The district across the line, vaguely visible through the pall, was the seat of a separate welter of noise and confusion that indicated festivities were at their usual high pitch.

Brazil took it all in with a probing, inclusive sweep of his eyes and then settled his attention on the Antlers Hotel, across the way and down a few doors. The shades had been drawn over the windows of the lower floor, and the wide door with its squares of colored glass was closed. There had been no trouble there yet, as he'd expected, but Moriah was overflowing with trail hands and likely, before many more hours had passed, that would change.

At once, Brazil spurred out into the open, and crossing the street, cut in behind Jergens', which stood on the corner, and rode on until he was behind the hostelry, standing next in the line of buildings.

A buggy was drawn up to the hitch rack, and glancing at it, Luke recognized the Box B brand of Ben Lockwood on the mare's hip. Kneeing his horse in beside it, he dismounted, and securing his animal to the crossbar, started for the rear door of the Antlers. In that moment two riders, coming from the weedy lot between Jergens' and the hotel, swung into view. Both slowed instantly as they saw Brazil, their sweaty, dusty features registering surprise when they noted the star pinned to his shirt pocket.

"Why, howdy, Marshal," one said thickly, after his moments of recovery. "We sure wasn't expecting to see you!"

Luke, one hand resting lightly on the butt of his pistol, nodded coolly. Somewhere along the street, glass shattered noisily as a window was destroyed.

"You're on the wrong side of the line," he said in a tight, clipped tone. "I want you back where you belong — fast."

The drovers stared at him woodenly for a long breath, and then one shrugged. "Sure," he said indifferently, and raking his horse with long-tined Mexican spurs, rushed off down the alley, his partner, swaying uncertainly on the saddle, a few strides behind him.

Brazil continued, gained the landing at the rear of the hotel, and reached for the doorknob. The panel was locked. Raising a fist, he hammered on the thick wood.

"Open up! It's the marshal!"

Almost at once, a narrow crack of light showed between the door and its facing. Carson, the hotel proprietor, peered out. "You the man the mayor was talking about?"

"I am," Brazil snapped, and pushed his way into the building. "Where's the Lockwoods?"

Carson, a thin, short man with gray hair and moustache, pointed toward the front of the structure. "In the parlor. You aiming to —"

Brazil, with time critical, ignored the man and hurried on down the narrow hallway to the lobby and turned into it. A dozen persons had gathered there, whiling away the minutes in nervous conversation, leafing through the yellowed pages of old magazines, or simply staring at the walls.

Jenny Lockwood rose to meet him as he halted in the center of the cluttered room. She was tall, attractive, and dressed in a white shirtwaist and full skirt; her hair appeared almost black and her eyes took on a deeper blue in the shadowy confines of the room. A smile of relief parted her lips as she moved toward him.

"Luke!" she murmured.

He caught her in his arms, his features tightening slightly at the display of affection. "You're all right," he said.

She nodded, drew back from him. "We've been afraid something might happen — those drovers. Mr. Carson thought they might try to force their way in. I was so relieved when the mayor came and said you'd be here soon."

"Best you get out of here in a hurry. I look for things to bust wide open as soon as it's full dark," Luke said, looking beyond her to Mrs. Lockwood, now on her feet, waiting quietly.

Jenny turned at once and crossed to her mother, a small, passive but unusually beautiful woman with a quiet, fixed smile. Taking up a parcel, the girl caught the older woman by the arm, and together they crossed to where Brazil waited.

"Out the back," he said, touching the brim of his hat to Mrs. Lockwood. "Your buggy's still there at the rack."

Jenny did not hesitate or voice any question, simply started down the hallway. Luke glanced at the others, watching him from their places in the lobby.

"Stay where you are," he said. "I'll be back shortly and quiet things down."

Moving on, he stepped past the two women, opened the door and had his searching look into the darkening area. There was no one around. Turning, he led Jenny and her mother to the buggy, handed them onto the seat, and stepping up to the rack, freed the horse.

Mrs. Lockwood smiled doubtfully at him. "Do — do you think it's safe?"

Brazil nodded, hearing a click behind him as Carson locked the door of the hotel. "I'll be riding with you until you're out of town. You won't be bothered."

The woman settled back. "Thank you — Luke," she said.

It was the first time Jenny's mother had ever addressed him by his first name. He glanced at the girl. She was smiling at him.

The racket in the street had increased —

guns cracking, hoofs pounding, dogs barking frantically. Jenny, taking up the reins, considered Brazil soberly.

"I'm not sure I like your taking over the marshal's job —"

"I don't mind helping out a bit," he said, turning to his horse. He did not explain that her safety and that of her mother had been the principal reason for stepping in to replace the dead lawman; it seemed unnecessary.

"I'm not sure I like the idea at all," Jenny continued, pausing to listen to the sounds in the street. "How can you — alone —"

"I'll be all right," Luke said. "I'd like for you to be out of here, however. Head on down the alley. I'll follow."

Jenny considered him for a brief moment, and then, slapping the mare with the reins, swung away from the rack. As the buggy cut sharply about and began to roll forward, Brazil mounted to his saddle, and spurring around, rode in beside it.

"Put the mare to a run," he said as Jenny turned to face him. "You can let her slow down once your ranch is in sight."

The girl signified her understanding. "We'll be fine once we're out of town," she said, and then again her features sobered. "Luke — you'll be careful —"

Brazil nodded, waved her on. "I make a habit of that," he said, raising his voice to be heard above the grating wheels and the thud of the horses. "Good night."

3

Brazil stayed near Jenny Lockwood and her mother for a long mile and then, certain there was no possibility of their encountering trouble, cut about and hurried back to the settlement.

Activity was continuing to heighten. There now appeared to be more men on the street, some riding, others walking, staggering, a few with bottles of whiskey clutched in hand as they prowled along the buildings.

Making certain the star he wore was clearly visible, Luke drew his pistol and, holding it in view in his lap, entered the street at its lower end. Guiding his horse into dead center of the roadway, he headed slowly for the marshal's office, near midway along the row of structures.

His arrival drew immediate attention.

Several trail hands paused to give his rigid, threatening shape close appraisal, and then, shrugging, began to drift leisurely back in the direction of the dead line. Others merely stared resentfully or ventured jeering comments, at which their companions laughed. Brazil made no response, simply maintained his course for the small building that housed the jail and lawman's office.

Reaching there, he holstered his weapon and veered into the alleyway that separated the building from its neighbor to the south: Mrs. Haskell's Boardinghouse, and drew to a stop at the hitch rack at the rear of the place. Dropping from the saddle, fully aware of the continuing racket and revelry in the street, he secured the bay he was riding, crossed to the back door of the jail, and entered.

"Hey, Marshal — why'n't you come on out and join us?"

The shout came from directly in front of the office. Luke paused beside the desk set at one end of the small room, glanced through the barred window. Four men, all obviously drunk. They were lounging against the crossbar of the rack erected in front of the building.

"Now, you ain't afeard of us, are you, Marshal? We're just a bunch of good old boys having us a time!"

"That's right, Marshal! Hell, we won't hurt you none!"

Luke stood for a long minute in the darkness of the room, considering the drovers. They were friendly drunk — not the mean, quarrelsome kind. But they could be a source of trouble if they continued to gulp down liquor at the rate they were.

Turning to the gunrack mounted on the wall of the lawman's office, Brazil reached for one of the shotguns. A chain, passed through the trigger guards and secured by a padlock and hasp, prevented the weapon's removal. Luke swore impatiently. The key to the lock could be anywhere.

"You acoming out, Marshal?"

Pivoting, Brazil crossed to the door, flung back the screen, and stepped out into the street. His abrupt appearance brought the drunks up short, laid a stillness upon them.

"I'm telling you men one time: I want you back across the line," Brazil snapped, glancing toward Jergens' store, where some sort of altercation was underway. "I don't want to spoil your fun by locking you up, but that's sure as hell what I'll do if you don't move on."

The drovers stared at him sullenly. One spat into the dust. "We ain't doing nothing wrong. Just having us a little sashay through the town," he protested.

"Maybe so, but you're not doing it on this side of the dead line. Get back over in Perdition."

Several gunshots racketed along the dark street, followed by the clatter of broken glass and much shouting and laughing. It came from the opposite end of town, from the row of small offices near Joe Adams' saloon, which stood on the corner.

"Take your choice, boys," Brazil stated abruptly. "The lockup or the other side of the line! I want to know what it's to be — right now."

"Well, I sure ain't honing to spend the

night in the calaboose," one of the riders replied hastily, wagging his head. "Come on, let's go."

All four of the men pulled away from the rack, moving unsteadily off down the street in the direction of Perdition. For a time, Brazil did not stir but kept his eyes on the quartet as some of the old caution slipped back into him, and then as the men continued on their way and shortly were lost in the darkness, he whirled on a heel and struck diagonally along the street for Jergens', where a fairly large crowd had now gathered.

He reached the mercantile store quickly and found several men engaged in a free-for-all in the pool of light being cast by lanterns the store's proprietor used to mark the entrance to his wagon yard. Not all bystanders were of the trail-hand crew, he noted; at least a half dozen watching were local men who had chosen to ignore his warning, through John Ashford, to stay off the street.

"Back off — all of you!" Luke shouted. Using his pistol as a club, he moved into the melee of heaving, swaying figures, all but obscured by the swirling dust.

The men broke apart, fell away, cursing, sweating, brushing at their clothing. One, angered and unthinking, surged toward the lawman. Brazil felled him with a sharp blow to the temple, and then, arms folded across his chest, calmly faced the others.

"Get across the line," he ordered, "and stay there."

A husky, red-shirted drover with blood crusting his lower lip, shook his head. "Maybe we ain't of the notion."

"Better get the notion," the lawman replied coldly. "Never did like killing a man for having a good time — but it's happened."

Coiled, waiting, eyes on the man ranged before him, Luke Brazil rode out the tense moments. Arkansas's cautioning words concerning the possibility that his skills with a sixgun had faded came back to him. Fully confident, Luke brushed them aside. Drawing fast, shooting accurately, were just part of the game; coolness of nerves and being able to judge an opponent, anticipate his thoughts, were equally important when it came to surviving in a shootout, and he knew he had not lapsed there. Perhaps he was a shade slower — he didn't really know — but nothing else had changed.

"What's it to be?" he said in a quiet, almost inviting way.

The red-shirted drover continued to glare at him through the settling dust for another long breath, and then he glanced at the men around him.

"Hell, we can have us a better time over at the Horsehead," he declared. "One of you give me a hand here with Curly, and let's get going."

The readiness in Luke Brazil began to ease. He took a step back, allowed his arms to drop to his sides. The local bystanders had begun to drift off into the shadows beyond the flare of lantern light, now that the attraction had ended. None had bothered to speak or in any way welcome or congratulate him; they had simply looked on and departed.

A hard half-smile pulled at Brazil's lips as he watched the drovers lift their stunned member to his feet and head toward the far end of town. Such treatment was not new to him; all too often, folks wanted a hard-nosed lawman to protect them and see to their welfare, but by the same token cared not to include him in their circle of friends. He reckoned he was doubly damned in the eyes of some, for not only was he the man who wore the star but an accursed bounty hunter as well — all of which actually accounted little to him. He had a life to live and he intended to live it according to the dictates of his own conscience and desires.

The drovers had reached Dead Ute Creek, making their way across the bridge for the noisy, well-lighted area beyond it. When they had passed from sight, Brazil stirred, retraced his steps back into the center of the roadway, and threw his glance along its length.

Things had quieted down considerably, and the number of drovers had dwindled. Evidently the word had spread among the trail hands, and now they would either obey the order to stay on the north side of the dead line — or they would gang up and come across to defy him. It was always difficult to anticipate just how a bunch of liquored-up men would react to authority.

Dropping back to the board sidewalk on the east side of the street, Brazil began to walk slowly toward the opposite end of the town. Shadowy figures along the way melted quietly into the passageways between the buildings or moved on as he approached, and the thought came to him that calming down Moriah might turn out to be a much less arduous task than he'd figured.

He reached the Antlers Hotel, paused to open the door, and looked inside. The lobby was deserted. Those who had taken refuge there earlier with Jenny and her mother evidently had deemed it safe to venture outside and make their way home.

He encountered a lone drover dozing on the steps at the side of the hotel, roused him, and sent him grumbling toward the dead line. Matters had not quieted any in Perdition, Luke noted as he watched the man's unsteady departure, but that was to be expected — and as it should be. Trail hands were entitled to blow off steam, and were welcome to do so as long as they stuck to the prescribed areas.

The first of the offices along the row, one occupied jointly by a land speculator and a surveyor, was in darkness. So also were the succeeding quarters of Doc Middleburg, lawyer Albert Koon, and the boot and shoe shop of Harry Vito, but as he drew abreast the latter, Brazil thought he caught the sound of a muffled cry.

Rigid, his shoulders a high, square line in the night, Brazil listened. The cry, more of a sob than anything else, seemed to have come from a small building, once occupied by a printer, that stood on the opposite side of the adjoining vacant lot.

The sound reached Luke again, and casting a glance at the front of the old structure, noting the closed door further secured by boards nailed diagonally across it, he stepped down off the sidewalk, and in the faint light of the stars and moon, hurried across the cleared ground and approached the building from the rear.

The door there was partly open, and as

Brazil drew in close, he heard scuffling and muttering. Drawing his pistol, he moved up to the opening. At once a dark shape emerged from the black interior to block his way.

"Get going!" a harsh voice ordered.

There was a sudden increase of frantic sounds and gasps from beyond the crouched figure. Brazil raised a hand, gave the man barring his path a shove to one side.

"Out of the way —"

The man rocked, caught himself. "Who the hell you think you are — busting in here on us and —"

"The marshal," Brazil cut in roughly, and swung his pistol hard against the drover's skull.

The figure staggered back, disappeared into the gloom that filled the store building. Darting inside quickly to avoid being silhouetted in the doorway, Brazil flattened himself against a wall. The scuffling noises had ceased, and there was now only the subdued sobbing of a woman to be heard. Anger soared through Luke as he realized what he had interrupted.

"Get out — all of you!" he snarled, and took a precautionary step to one side. He could see dim shapes in the blackness; two men — three counting the one he had knocked down. The woman was somewhere on the floor, he reckoned, since he could not locate her.

A dark shape blocked the doorway, immediately disappeared. Another followed, crowding the first closely as he made his hasty departure. There was no response from the third. Brazil moved again, tension rising within him. He hadn't hit the man that hard.

"You — move out!" he barked, and once more changed position.

Boot heels scraped on the dry, wooden floor. A third shadowy figure filled the entrance to the old print shop for a brief instant, and was gone. The lawman's taut shape relented. He shifted his attention to the center of the room.

"It's all right, they're gone," he said. "I'm the marshal."

At once a slight figure sprang erect and rushed for the doorway. It was one of

Aaron Horn's daughters, Luke saw as the girl reached the pale light outside the building. Evidently she had been caught on the street as night settled over the town, being abroad for some reason, had been trapped by the three drovers and carried into the empty storeroom. Now, understandably, she was making every effort to conceal her identity from him.

With the sound of her hurrying footsteps in his ears as she hurried for home, Brazil holstered his pistol and crossed to the door. Hesitating there briefly, and hearing nothing to alarm him, he stepped back out into the alley. Instantly he rocked to one side, the faint glint of starshine on metal sending its warning to him.

Directly in front of him a pistol blasted, the muzzle flash illuminating the night for an instant of time. One of the drovers he'd driven off — likely the one he'd buffaloed. Brazil was barely conscious of the thought as he drew and fired at the powder flare.

He heard the man grunt in pain as the bullet ripped into him. From off a few steps to the right a voice yelled, "He's shot Garret," and then came the quick rap of running feet as the two other drovers beat a hasty retreat for the dead line.

The gunshots had apparently gone unnoticed, but Brazil, cautioned by experience, moved quickly away from the wall of the empty building and halted in a pool of blackness at its side. In the weak light he saw the drover, pistol clutched in his hand, lying face down in the dust of the alley. After a moment he crossed to where Garret lay. It took but a brief examination to see that he was dead.

Grim, Luke wrenched the pistol from Garret's stiffening fingers, thrust it under his own belt, and drew himself upright. This could bring matters to a swift and violent head. As long as there was no killing, a crew of hard-case drovers usually could be controlled, but let one of their number meet death at the hands of either a civilian or a lawman and the entire band was likely to come seeking vengeance.

The wise thing was to make the first move, one calculated to set them all back on their heels, blunt their intentions.

45

Brazil turned, and angling across the vacant lot, crossed the street to the marshal's office.

A dark shape slouched in the chair near the desk sent the lawman's hand dropping to the butt of his pistol.

"It's only me," Arkansas said hastily.

Luke swore. "You fresh out of matches? Why the hell didn't you light a lamp?"

The older man, his earlier, disapproving attitude changed, laughed. "You're touchy as a turpentined cat! Happens I ain't running the place, and I figured if you wanted it lit up you would've done it yourself. . . . You got bad trouble?" he added, looking more closely at Brazil as the lawman touched the wick of a lamp with flame and filled the room with a warm, yellow glow.

Luke, relieving himself of Garret's weapon, stepped to the window, pulled down the shade, and kicked the door shut with a heel. "Had to kill one of Sobel's drovers."

Arkansas whistled softly.

"Had no choice," Brazil said. "Found

three of them had grabbed themselves a girl and carried her into that empty building near the shoe shop. One of them — name was Garret — took a shot at me."

The older man was wagging his head slowly. "Sure could start things to popping. The girl all right?"

Luke had turned to the desk, searching the drawers for a key to the gunrack. Finding a ring with several, he crossed to the padlock, began a trial and error system in an effort to find one that fit.

"I don't know. She didn't wait to talk."

"You know who she was?"

The third key opened the thick lock. Brazil let the chain drop, selected one of the shotguns. "I'm not sure," he said. "Too dark."

Arkansas nodded, pressing the question no further. "What're you aiming to do about that drover?"

"The two with Garret lit out for Perdition after they saw him go down. They'll be carrying the tale to Sobel and the rest of the crew. I'm going to head them off if they've got some ideas of coming here after me."

Arkansas got to his feet, and turning to the wall rack, chose a shotgun for his own use. "Think I'll just trot along with you."

Brazil, having loaded the double-barreled weapon he'd picked, was stuffing extra shells into a side pocket.

"I'll appreciate it," he said, "but there's no call for you to stick out your neck."

"Expect there ain't, only I am," the older man replied, helping himself to the cartridges. "You got some scheme in mind?"

"I'm going to load Garret up on my horse, hand him over to Sobel — he's still laying out there back of that storeroom. But first I want to get all of those trail hands over where they belong. Got most of them off the street, but there's still a few hanging around."

Arkansas nodded. "Seen a couple or so in the restaurant when I come in. There's a bunch in Joe Adams' saloon, too."

"There'll be others turning up once we start looking. We'll drop back to the end

48

of the street, work this way. Means going into every building that's open, and chousing out the passageways, too . . . Better pin one of those deputy badges on."

Arkansas picked up one of the stars lying on the desk, affixed it to his vest pocket, and moved toward the door. "Some of them counterjumpers ain't exactly going to be happy with us chasing off their business."

"Might call it business now, but in a couple more hours they'll be thinking something else," Luke said, stepping out into the street. "They want peace and quiet — that's what they're going to get."

"Amen," Arkansas murmured and fell in behind the lawman.

Side by side, guns hanging from the crooks of their arms, they walked to the upper end of Moriah's single street. There, separating, Arkansas taking the east side, Luke the west, they started back. The town had all but settled down, most of the drovers having gotten the message after earlier brushes with Brazil, but there were still a few stragglers and reluctants.

In the Palace Saloon Luke found three of the crew playing poker. He broke up the game, and under the hostile but silent attention of Alec Gruman, the proprietor, shepherded them out into the open and headed them for the dead line — all three mumbling threats as they departed.

In the restaurant next to the Palace he encountered two more, just finishing a meal, and quickly sent them along in the wake of the others. On the opposite side of the street Luke saw Arkansas root out a couple from alongside the hotel, where, for some unknown reason, they had been waiting.

He flushed out a lone drover hanging around Rankin's Gun & Saddle Shop and sent him on his way. Brazil's actions brought sharp, reproving words from Avery Rankin, but the lawman only shrugged and continued his slow, methodic patrol.

Ashford's was the last store in that side of the street, and reaching it, Luke found the place dark and the door locked. Evidently the mayor preferred not to run the risk of having any of the trail drivers as customers.

Directly opposite was Joe Adams' saloon, and crossing over, Brazil pushed through the batwing doors, finding Arkansas already there. Two drovers were standing at the bar, considering the older man with a look of curling contempt on their wind-curried faces. As Luke moved into view their attitudes altered immediately, and tossing off their drinks they paid the bartender and returned to the street.

Adams, not liking it at all, came out from behind the counter, his square, florid face working with anger.

"This ain't right!" he stormed. "You're running off cash customers! You ain't the marshal, anyway."

Brazil had motioned to Arkansas to keep an eye on the drovers, make certain they had gone on over the line. He nodded to Adams, shrugged.

"Ashford's orders were to get that bunch out of town and back where they belong. That's what we're doing. If you don't like it, go talk to him."

"By God, that's what I'm going to

do!'' Adams shouted. ''Money ain't so plentiful around here that I can afford to throw it away.''

''Talk to the mayor,'' Brazil repeated calmly, and wheeled to the swinging doors.

Stepping out into the cool, dry evening, he rejoined Arkansas. The two drovers had crossed over Dead Ute Creek and were disappearing into the haze of dust that hung over Perdition.

''Reckon that does it,'' the older man said. ''What's coming next?''

''We go get the horses and pay a little visit to Parley Sobel and his bunch. Got a dead man I want to hand over to them.''

4

With Garret's body draped across the skirt of his saddle and Arkansas at his side, Luke Brazil rode through the scatter of men gathered in front of the saloons in Perdition and halted at the rack fronting the largest one, the Horsehead. Sobel and most of his men would be inside it.

Dismounting, Luke waited until Arkansas had swung down and moved to his side. Then, handing the older man his double-barreled weapon, he slung Garret over his shoulder, mounted the two steps leading up to the porch, and crossing, entered the crowded, smoke-filled room.

The hubbub began to fade immediately, and as the quiet grew, the lawman walked directly to the nearest table, and ignoring the two men sitting at it, laid the body of the drover upon it. Behind him, just inside the doorway, Arkansas, a cocked shotgun braced and ready under each arm, was keeping a wary eye not only on the startled patrons but on the bystanders collecting outside on the porch as well.

Dropping back a few steps to where he could face the entire crowd, Brazil let his glance sweep the gathering.

"Which one of you's Sobel?" he asked.

From off to one side a tall, dark man with a heavy, sweeping mustache and a thick, bull neck drew himself erect.

"That's me —"

"Man there's Garret," the lawman said, jerking a thumb at the drover. "Expect he works for you —"

"He does," the rancher cut in. "I know all about you shooting him down."

"His friends brought the word. Reckon you know how it happened then, too."

"Slim and Rufe said you shot him down — that's all I know and all that matters," Sobel stated coldly. "And you best hear this: no tinhorn marshal's going to get away with killing one of my boys!"

A mutter of approval came from the room. Over beyond Sobel Luke could see the owner of the Horsehead, Jed Tillman, watching and listening. Tillman was no friend of his, had not been since the saloon man and two of his gamblers had teamed up to fleece Earl Dutton, one of his cowhands, out of a month's wages and Brazil had gone in and forcibly recovered the cash.

"He won't be the last," the lawman said evenly, "unless you all stick to the rules. You know what they are, Sobel, and if you don't or maybe've forgot, I'll repeat them. Keep your —"

"Don't go wasting your breath. I know."

"Then, stick to them. That goes not only for your bunch but everybody else around here: you're welcome across the dead line during daylight hours — if you're sober and behave yourself. Otherwise keep out — and it's my job to see that you do."

"Was that other tin star's job too, only he ain't around no more," a voice in the back of the room said.

"Well, I am," Brazil countered flatly.

Parley Sobel suddenly was angry. He

swiped at the sweat on his leathery face, shook his head, and glared at Brazil.

"Just who the hell you think you're talking to? I can buy and sell you a half a dozen times was I to take the notion. Now, I don't take that kind of lip from nobody!"

"You're taking it from me," Luke replied in his cool, even way. "And if you'd like to argue the point why, I'm feeling just right — and this here's as good a place as any."

The silence in the Horsehead had deepened, and the hot, smoke-choked air was stifling. Sobel licked at his lips, frowned, and glanced about at the men gathered around him, waiting for a move of some sort on his part.

The moment was ripe for wholesale slaughter; the cattleman had but to give the word and his trail hands would go for their weapons. But Sobel was no fool. He was respecting the tall, hard-featured man standing, coiled to strike, in the front of the room, and the two shotguns, their rabbit-ear hammers pulled to full cock, being held by the deputy just inside the door — if not the badges they wore.

"This ain't the place to settle this," he said, shrugging.

"Up to you —"

"Maybe so, but there'll come another time. Too many folks in here. Some of them could get hurt."

Brazil laughed, the sound dry, mocking. "Sure, sure. Folks mean a lot to you," he said. Backing slowly, he returned to where Arkansas waited and reclaimed his shotgun. "I want to know when you're pulling out."

Parley Sobel's broad face flared with anger again. "You running us off?"

Before Luke could reply, Jed Tillman rushed forward to take a position at the side of the cattleman. Anger gripped him also as he raised an arm, shook a finger at the lawman.

"Goddammit, Brazil — you ain't got the right to do this! These here are my customers and I won't stand for you ordering them to move on."

"Far as the town's concerned, you've already been run off," Luke said to Sobel, coolly ignoring the saloon man's protests.

"Garret there fixed that up good for you. You and your bunch can hang around on this side of the dead line till hell freezes over if you want — just don't cross over."

"Had some buying I aimed to do —"

"Forget it. Too late for that now. I'm asking when you're leaving so's I'll know how much longer I'll have to keep this shotgun loaded."

"Figuring to pull out in the morning," Sobel said finally, a reluctance in his voice.

"I'll be looking forward to it," Brazil said caustically, and hanging the shotgun in the bend of his elbow, pivoted and stepped back out onto the porch.

He halted there, hearing Arkansas again move in behind him, facing the small crowd who had gathered to witness the proceedings inside the Horsehead. Several drovers, cowhands, women, a couple of gamblers from Long John Green's saloon; Sam Hester, owner of the Texas Alamo, another of Perdition's saloons; Ed Steele, who ran the restaurant that adjoined Tillman's Horsehead.

"I make myself clear in there?" Luke asked, glancing around. "That goes for everybody."

Steele, a lean, angular man with a pointed beard, turned his head to the side, spat. "You was mighty high-handed in there, way I see it," he said. "And you ain't even the real marshal."

"I'll do till one comes along," Brazil snapped. "Anybody else got anything to say?"

There was no response. Nodding crisply, Luke moved on off the porch and crossed to where the horses were waiting. Mounting up, he sat quietly, shotgun still held at readiness while Arkansas swung onto his saddle, and then together they cut quickly back into the darkness beyond the flaring circle of lamplight.

"That was a mite close there for a bit," Arkansas murmured as they reached the bridge spanning Dead Ute Creek and started across. "Didn't think that there Sobel fellow was going to back down — not with all the help he had."

"Surprised me some, too. Expect he didn't like looking at the business end of these shotguns. Something about the size of the holes and thinking about all that buckshot coming out that sort of curls a man's backbone.''

"For certain," Arkansas said, glancing over his shoulder. "Expect he figured he was first in line, too, for a full charge. You think we've heard the last of it from him?''

"Hard to say," Brazil replied as they veered toward the jail. The town was quiet now, and all of the store windows were dark. Only the lamps at the Palace Saloon and Joe Adams' place were alight. Even the lanterns that ordinarily glowed at the entrance to McKenzie's Livery Stable were off.

"Kind of showed him up in front of his crew," Arkansas said doubtfully. "That ain't going to set good with him."

Brazil showed little interest. "His problem," he said as they drew up to the hitch rack. "Obliged to you for siding me."

"We done for the night?''

Brazil nodded, came down off his saddle. "I'd like for you to ride on to the ranch, see that things get taken care of there. You can come back in the morning."

"Sure. I forgot to ask, we was so busy first off, but was the lady and her ma all right when you rode in?"

"Fine. I loaded them up in their buggy and put them on the way home. . . . You mind leaving my horse at McKenzie's as you go by?"

"Nope," the older man said, taking the bay's reins from Luke's hand. "What'll you be doing the rest of the night?"

"Going to set myself here in the office, wait for daylight. Sobel said they'd be leaving then. I want to be on hand when they do."

"Yeh, I'm wondering about him and his bunch. Seems it was all mighty easy back there. You certain it's a good idea you staying here alone? Them drovers could get it into their heads to do something about that there friend of theirs you put a bullet into."

"I doubt it," the lawman said, moving toward the door to his office. "See you in the morning."

"G'night," Arkansas replied, and wheeling away from the rack, moved off down the street.

Luke, stepping up into the doorway, paused and threw his glance toward Perdition. There had been no diminishing of noise and light there, and the haze of dust still hung over the squat buildings and the plaza area fronting them like a yellow cloud.

Abruptly he straightened, attention centering on two men silhouetted briefly against the glow as they crossed Dead Ute Creek. They were avoiding the bridge, wading the stream, as if wishing to conceal their movements.

Arkansas could be right. Trouble could be on the way. Some of Garret's friends might be taking it on themselves to square accounts for him. The lawman came around hurriedly. Arkansas was well down the street. Luke shrugged it off. There was no sense calling him; the men fording the creek could mean nothing.

Brazil moved on into the office, going first to the lamp, barely alive. The oil was gone, he noted, and blowing out the last

62

tiny flame, he lit a second fixture, one standing on a table well back in a corner. Arkansas had retained the shotgun he had carried, and Luke, taking up the one he had placed inside the door as he entered, returned it to the rack.

He hesitated, a frown pulling together his thick eyebrows. Two men fording the creek when the bridge was only a few steps away didn't fit. There had to be a reason. On sudden impulse, Brazil reached out, lowered the wick in the lamp he'd just lit to reduce the flare of light, and cutting back through the jail, went out the rear. There he quickly circled the building to the passageway lying between it and the adjacent boardinghouse and hurried along its dark, littered length to the street. Leaning up against a wall, well in the shadows, he waited.

Within only minutes Luke heard the faint, dry scrape of boots on the sidewalk somewhere down the way — in front of Rankin's, he thought. Motionless, a hard-cornered smile breaking his taut lips, he realized he had been right, after all. He listened, eyes straining to pierce the night.

"Rufe — you see him?"

Rufe. . . . One of Garret's friends. The other man, the one who had just whispered, would be Slim.

"Can't see nothing. Damn lamps down low. Ain't sure whether that's him setting in the corner or it's something on a chair."

The pair had worked forward tight against the wall, crouched. Rufe was in front of Slim, endeavoring to get a good look into the office area of the jail.

"He's in there somewheres," Slim muttered hoarsely. "We seen him go in."

"I'm betting he's back in one of them cells," Rufe said. "Gone and crawled onto a cot and's getting hisself some shut-eye."

Brazil, moving silently, pulled away from the wall of the boardinghouse, and still in the deep shadows, circled in behind the two drovers.

"Just about where he is," Slim agreed. "Be like shooting fish in a barrel, was we to find him there."

"Ain't no other place he can be," Rufe replied, irritably. "Let's have us a look-see."

Luke watched the pair creep forward, gain the doorway, and walking carefully to avoid making noise, step into the office. At that moment the lawman closed in.

"Hold it right where you are!" he snapped, coming into the room.

The two men froze, raising their hands slowly. Rufe swore, muttering something under his breath. Brazil, leveled pistol in one hand, relieved them of their weapons and pulled back.

"Cells are on down the hall," he said. "Get in the first one you come to."

Slim started at once to make his way along the narrow, dimly lit corridor, but Rufe hung back. "Sobel ain't going to like this — you locking us up —"

"I don't give a damn what Sobel likes!" Luke stated in a flat voice. "Move — or I'll lay this sixgun along the side of your head!"

Rufe swore again but immediately followed his friend into the first cell. Brazil, taking the keys off their peg, slammed the grill door shut and locked it.

"How long you keeping us here?"

Rufe demanded.

"Depends," the lawman said vaguely and, pivoting, made his way back to the office.

As he returned the keys to their customary place, he could hear the two drovers talking in low voices. There could be more of them involved, he decided; best he take precautions.

Wheeling once more, he hurried down the hallway to the back door, dropped the crossbar into its brackets, and secured it from outside entry. Following a like procedure at the front, he dragged a chair around to where he would be facing the street, and settling down, blew out the lamp. Within only moments he was asleep.

5

Yells, the thunder of running horses, and the crackle of gunshots brought Luke Brazil awake with a start. Lunging to his feet, he rushed to the window, pulled aside the shade, and looked out into the street. Riders were streaming by.

It was Parley Sobel's crew. They were demonstrating their contempt for him, and the town, by creating as much of a disturbance as possible in their departure. Brazil watched them race by, hearing, above the drumming of hoofs and shouts, the excited barking of dogs and an occasional clatter of metal or the crash of glass as a bullet found its target. Anger lifting within him, he scanned the noisy cavalcade for Sobel. The cattleman wasn't among them, unless he had been in the lead, and that wasn't likely.

A hard smile crossed Luke Brazil's mouth as suspicion filled his mind. Evidently Sobel was going to have his moment after all — so he figured. Pulling on his hat, briefly checking his pistol, Luke pivoted and headed down the hallway for the rear door. Ignoring the demands of Rufe and Slim that they be released, he removed the crossbar, opened the thick panel, and stepped out into the cool first light.

Crossing behind the jail, he continued along the back of the structures lining that side of the street until he reached Hans Schulte's meat market. There he cut left along the low, squat building and made his way to its front corner, stopping just short of the sidewalk.

Careful to keep back, he let his glance probe the opposite side of the roadway. A grim smile cracked his lips again. He hadn't been wrong.

Visible through the layers of floating dust churned up by the horses, crouched against the side of the Antlers Hotel, were three men: Parley Sobel and two of his drovers. Pistols drawn, they were watching the front of the jail closely, apparently expecting him to come bursting out of the doorway in angry response to the commotion being created by the crew as they rode out.

Arms folded, Brazil waited while the tan haze in the street slowly settled, and then as the hammer of hoofs and the barking of the dogs faded, he stepped out onto the sidewalk.

"Looking for me, Sobel?"

The cattleman and his two friends whirled, swinging their attention from the jail to the mouth of the passageway some fifty feet or so below. Surprise blanked their features, leaving them voiceless.

People were appearing along the street, roused by the horses and the shooting and yelling. Some were standing on the landing fronting their places of business, others were on the sidewalks staring off to the south, the direction into which Sobel's trail hands had vanished. At Luke's words, many turned to him and to the three men facing the lawman from the opposite side of the street.

Sobel made no reply. After a few

moments he dropped his pistol back into its holster, nodded resignedly to the man standing at his left, who wheeled immediately, and cut back along the side of the hotel. His plan to bushwhack Brazil had failed, and it was clear he had no wish to pursue it further on an even basis despite the fact that he had two men backing his play.

"I'm still here, Sobel," Luke called.

The cattleman's shoulders shifted. "I'm letting it ride," he said.

A tense hush, broken only by the distant lowing of a cow somewhere back in the residential area, had fallen over the town. The sky above the horizon to the east had paled, and the first hint of the rising sun showed in streaks of color shooting fanlike up into the vast arch of pearl gray.

Brazil was a tall, square-shouldered figure standing boldly out in the open. He appeared loose, at ease, yet there was a coiled quality to him as if he were capable of springing into instantaneous action if necessary. He was still wearing the range clothing he had on when John Ashford and the two other townsmen had called upon him: stovepipe boots, cord pants tucked inside, faded blue linsey-woolsey shirt, vest, bandanna, and wide-brimmed, high-crowned, peaked hat.

A dark shadow of beard covered his cheeks and chin, and his full mustache looked black in the cold light, while his pale eyes appeared even a less definite shade. Unmoving, he continued to face Sobel and his man as if still hoping some move on their part would be made.

The second rider returned, leading the horses. He passed the reins of one to Parley Sobel, who immediately thrust a foot into a stirrup and heaved himself onto the saddle. The two crew members mounted also but hung back a few steps behind the cattleman.

"Ain't forgetting what you done, Marshal," Sobel called. "Ain't nobody guns down one of my boys without paying for doing it."

"You came close to losing a couple more last night," Brazil said. "I've got them locked up in my jail now —"

"Rufe and Slim — that's who he's

talking about," the rider to Sobel's left shouted. "That's what become of them!"

The cattleman nodded, studied Luke. "What're you aiming to do with them?"

"I'll figure something out."

"I can call back my boys, and break into that cracker box you call a jail."

"You can sure try," Brazil said with a humorless smile. "Yes sir, you can sure try."

Parley Sobel gave that consideration. "I reckon Rufe and Slim can take care of themselves," he said after a time. "Anyways, this ain't over. We'll be back —"

"No you ain't!" a voice shouted from a short distance down the walk. "You ain't never going to come here again!"

Brazil broke his fixed attention on Sobel and his men, swung it to the figure running out into the street. It was Aaron Horn. The clothing-store merchant was carrying a shotgun in one hand. He halted in front of Sobel, shook a finger at the rancher.

"This here's the last time you and your bunch are ever riding into this town — I promise you that! We don't want your kind around here no more!''

Sobel was looking down at Aaron, a half smile on his face. "You're talking mighty big for a little fellow," he said.

"I mean what I'm saying. When it gets to where the street ain't safe for our womenfolk then it's time to put a stop to the cause of it —"

"That goes for me, too," another man cut in, stepping off the walk into the loose dust of the street. It was Pete Spears, owner of the Star Restaurant. "Place of mine's a wreck — busted window, hitch rack tore down, sign all shot full of holes. You and your kind ain't welcome around here no more, Sobel."

The cattleman spat. "I reckon we'll come and go as we please."

"Not here you won't!" Horn shouted, thin, seamy face contorted with fury. "You ever show up in this town again, I'll blow your head off with this here shotgun!"

"Maybe you'd like to have a try right now," Sobel said, dropping a hand onto his pistol.

"Forget it!" Luke Brazil cut in sharply and moved farther into the street. "Horn, you and Spears go on about your business. Sobel — I want you out of here now!"

"Not till I've had my say!" a new voice broke in from behind the lawman.

Brazil swore feelingly in exasperation. It was Avery Rankin. He shook his head warningly at the gun-and-saddle-shop owner. The moments were taut, filled with tension and suppressed violence. The slightest spark could set off a killing.

"Back off, Rankin," the lawman ordered. "You can all talk this out later."

"No, I'm saying what I think now! I want Sobel to know this: that the whole town don't feel the way Horn and Spears — and maybe you — do. There's plenty of us appreciate the business we get from the drovers, and far as we're concerned, they're welcome here anytime."

"The hell they are!" Horn yelled and started toward Rankin.

Brazil quickly stepped out in front of the merchant, blocked him. "This ends right here," he said harshly, and swung his eyes to Sobel. "Ride out — now!"

The cattleman nodded coldly. "Sure, Marshal, but this ain't over between me and you yet. I want you to remember that."

"You know where to find me," Brazil replied, equally cold.

"What about Slim and Rufe?"

"They'll be along," Luke replied. "I don't want them in my jail any more than you do."

"I'm glad we agree on one thing," Sobel said dryly, and clucking to his horse, moved off into the street.

6

Luke Brazil watched Sobel and his men lope off through the thin sheen of dust still hanging between the two rows of buildings, all glancing from side to side as they passed the scatter of residents on the way. The smirk on their faces was evident, and it was clear they were enjoying the disturbance they had raised.

"Marshal —"

Luke brought his attention around. It was Avery Rankin. Dark, in his mid-thirties, he showed his anger in his eyes.

"I don't figure you've got any call to be taking sides against folks doing business with us here in town."

"I'm not," Brazil stated flatly. "I was asked to step in and keep the peace. I did it the only way I know how."

"By running off cash customers! Hell, I

was figuring to do a good business with Sobel's boys this morning before they headed back to Texas, but you drove them off.''

''And it's a good thing he did!'' Aaron Horn shouted, catching a bit of the conversation and hurrying up. ''There'd've been some killings right here in the street if they'd started in hoorawing and deviling us again. I don't ever want to see a goddam trail hand again —''

''*You* don't want!'' Rankin echoed. ''Just who the hell you think you are, saying what's what for the whole town! You got some idea you're the only man in business in Moriah?''

''Both of you — settle down!'' Brazil broke in sternly, anxious to close the argument between the two men before it mounted to serious proportions. ''You can thrash it out with the mayor,'' he added, ducking his head toward John Ashford approaching at a fast walk with several other merchants.

Horn turned to the newcomers. ''Expect you'll find them all siding in with me. Hell, any fool can see we've got to put a stop to them wild, filthy drovers coming here. Look at the town! A man'd think a cyclone had struck it.''

Understandably, Aaron Horn was making no mention of the ordeal that his daughter had been put through, but there was no doubt that knowledge of it was the underlying reason for the militant attitude he had assumed.

Moriah was a shambles, Brazil had to agree. Windows broken, signs badly damaged by bullets — some hanging drunkenly from one support, others down entirely in the dust. Most of the hitch racks had been jerked out of the ground by playful trail hands practicing with their ropes, and the water trough at McKenzie's Livery Stable had been overturned.

The body of a dog lay half in, half out of the passageway between Ashford's and Rankin's, where it had apparently fled in a futile attempt to escape a trigger-happy drover, and in the vacant lot east of the school a wagon lay on its side.

"And that ain't the worst of it!" Horn said, raising his voice to be heard by all along the street. "It's what's happening to folks living here. Old man Evans got hit in the leg by a stray bullet, and I heard that Mex family living up along the creek got their garden all ruined. A bunch of them hellions rode their horses into their crops, tromping the melons and the corn and stuff just for cussedness. Fellow tried to stop them, got a wallop on the head for his trouble."

"And we best not be forgetting it was one of them that fired the bullet that killed Jesse Hurley," Pete Spears added. "Let's don't be forgetting that!"

"No, sir, we sure better not! Ain't nobody safe on the street when they're around — and it's just got to stop, that's all there is to it," Horn declared, and bobbed agitatedly to Ashford. "I reckon you'll agree with me on that, John."

Moriah's mayor had not taken time to dress completely, and lacked his usual collar and tie. The men with him — Alec Gruman, young owner of the Palace Saloon; general store proprietor Caleb Jergens; attorney Albert Koon; and thick-set Hans Schulte, the butcher — also appeared to have come in haste, summoned no doubt by the pitch of the loud voices in the street.

"I don't know what-all you've said, Aaron," Ashford replied soothingly, "but I did hear you tell Parley Sobel that he and his men weren't welcome here."

"And I told Horn he was talking out of turn!" Rankin said hurriedly. "He ain't speaking for the whole town!"

Schulte ran a heavy hand over his round, florid face. "It is bad when they are here," he said wearily in his thickly accented voice. "It is hard to make a living because of the damage —"

"Maybe so, but we need them just the same," Caleb Jergens said with a shake of his head. "Not only Parley Sobel's crew but all the others we can get. Drovers spend hard cash money, and it's their business that carries a lot of us through the slack months. Some of us would go broke if it wasn't for them."

"You're going to go broke anyway, paying for all they steal and for the damage they do!" Horn shouted, shaking a finger in Jergens' face. "By the time summer's over and the last bunch of them's come and gone you'll have lost all your profit fixing things up at your store — and that won't be counting what was stole."

"They don't get away with much that counts!" Jergens countered, "and it's sure no big trouble for me to take a hammer and nails and do some repairing —"

Ashford raised his hands, staying the angry words being thrown back and forth. "There's good sense in what you're both saying — and we need to talk it out. I —" The mayor paused, gaze settling at the end of the street, where three riders had swung into view. "Expect Ben Lockwood'll want to say something on the subject too. His missus and daughter got caught in town yesterday when things were so bad."

Luke, standing silently by, listening to what was being said, put his attention on the approaching men. Lockwood, a large, robust man with iron-gray hair and drooping mustache, sat forward on his saddle. His features were set to hard angles, and there was a belligerent pitch to his shoulders.

To his left was his son, Dave, not yet

out of his teen years but doing his best to live up to his father's expectations. The third rider was Enos Draper, the elderly owner of the ranch adjoining Lockwood's vast Box B spread and known to be beholden to the rancher.

The horsemen swung into the rack standing half upright in front of Doc Middleburg's office and dismounted. Both Lockwoods tossed their lines to Draper for securing and stalked up to the group of men awaiting them quietly.

"John," Ben Lockwood said with no preliminaries, "I got something to say. I want this town closed to trail herds. Yesterday my missus and daughter —"

"Just what we're talking about, Ben!" Aaron Horn broke in. "We're all wanting that."

"No, by God — not everybody!" Rankin shouted, surging toward the clothing-store merchant. "You ain't —"

Ashford waved the man back, raised his hands again to still the quick flow of hot words. He nodded to Lockwood.

"Morning, Ben. We've just been hashing that over. Some of the businessmen think it would be a good idea to do just that. Some don't."

Brazil watched the big rancher with dry amusement. Neither he nor his son Dave had troubled to speak or in any way acknowledge his presence. Because of his past, Lockwood disapproved of him as a possible son-in-law, Luke knew, but he gave that little thought. Jenny, while admiring and respecting her father, had a mind and a will of her own; she would do what she pleased when the time came.

"I don't see that there's any question about it —"

"Neither do I," Enos Draper said, coming up to take a position beside Lockwood. "We don't need all them outlaws and saddle tramps running loose around here."

"Yeh, you can say that, Enos!" Rankin protested in a bitter voice. "You don't have to depend on customers. You just have to drive your cows in to the spur, load them up — and you're done! Ones of us in business here, with all we've got sunk into whatever we're selling, have to grub out a living the whole year around."

"Or try, anyway," Caleb Jergens amended.

"It's my town, too," Draper insisted. "I've got a right to talk up. My womenfolk do their trading here and when them trail hands are all over the place they can't — they just have to stay home."

"It's getting to where it lasts all summer long, too," Aaron Horn said. "Used to be only three, maybe four herds was drove in — now there's a dozen or more outfits coming —"

"And we ain't seen the worst of them, either," Pete Spears said heavily, swiping at the sweat on his face with a forearm. "Cody Hungerford and his bunch ain't showed up yet."

Hungerford. . . . Brazil saw Ben Lockwood's jaw tighten and a hard glint come into his eyes at the mention of the name. Brazil knew the man only by reputation. Owner of a two-hundred-thousand-acre spread somewhere in southeastern New Mexico, Cody Hungerford ruled that part of the territory with ruthless autocracy.

It was said that even he didn't know

how many head of cattle he ran, but annually three thousand Hungerford steers were driven into the pens at Moriah for loading and shipment to eastern markets —not because he needed the money but because he had to thin out his herds.

The men who rode for him were of a special breed: Mexican *vaqueros,* renegades avoiding the law, hard-case trail drivers unable to work for the average rancher, and all others willing to trade loyalty and allegiance to an iron-handed boss who not only guaranteed them protection from all comers but paid top wages as well.

That previous year, Luke recalled, Hungerford's crew pretty well kept themselves in Perdition, thanks to the efforts of Town Marshal Jesse Hurley. The word was that Cody Hungerford owed the old lawman and that was his way of repaying.

Whatever, Moriah suffered only minor damage from the thirty or forty drovers that the rancher employed to push his herd — which was in marked contrast to previous times, when his men had left the settlement in much the same condition as had Parley Sobel's.

"When you reckon he'll be coming in?" Rankin wondered. Even the gun-and-saddle man was subdued at the thought of Hungerford's crew.

"Heard one of Sobel's bunch say they was a couple or three days ahead of them."

"Means we've got time enough to head them off," Ben Lockwood said briskly.

For reasons no one knew, there was bad blood between Lockwood and Cody Hungerford, and the feeling was so intense that the two men avoided each other scrupulously. It was as if each feared the consequences should they ever meet face to face. It was common knowledge that both had come originally from the same part of Texas, but there all information ended.

"We can't just up and do that, Ben," John Ashford said, frowning. "The man's been on the trail for weeks pushing his cattle. He's expecting to stop here, got his plans made for it. We can't ride out there and tell him to keep on going."

"Why not?" Lockwood demanded.

Alex Gruman smiled wryly. "You want the job, Ben? I sure don't!"

"It's not up to me," the rancher said, and finally taking note of Luke, added, "It'd be up to Brazil there, since he's taking on Hurley's badge."

"That's not the point," Ashford said; "it wouldn't be right. And while I'm thinking of it I'd like to say we owe Brazil a vote of thanks for taking over Jesse Hurley's job. The town would be in a lot worse shape than it is if he hadn't stepped in."

There was a murmur of agreement. Jergens said, "I ain't heard *you* say what you think about the trail herds, Luke. You for letting them come in?"

Brazil said, "Can't see as my opinion counts for much, but you're going to have to make a choice, far as I can see. Either the town gets along with the drovers — or it gets along without them."

"That ain't much help," Pete Spears said. "We already know that."

"Expect you do, but you need to make a decision, not just yammer it back and forth. Get everybody together, talk it over, and make up your minds.''

''Vote on it — that what you're saying?'' Gruman asked.

''I don't see any sense in that,'' Ben Lockwood declared, shaking his head. ''It's up to the businessmen and the ranchers.''

''Everybody'll be affected,'' Moriah's mayor said. ''I'm not sure your way's right, Ben.''

''Well, I am,'' the rancher snapped, glancing at Enos Draper, who was bobbing in agreement. ''It's wrong to leave important things like that to everybody. Most of them have an ax to grind and they're going to lag for what helps them the most.''

''And you ain't figuring that way?'' Jergens said in a sarcastic tone.

''I'm trying to figure what's best for the town,'' Lockwood replied. ''Don't be forgetting I ain't in business here, so tearing up the place don't mean nothing to me — I don't have to lay out a lot of cash on repairs and such. It's that I don't like seeing women and kids getting hurt.

"My wife and daughter came close to that only yesterday. They had to run and hide in the Antlers to keep out of the way of them damned renegades." Lockwood paused, jerking a thumb at Luke. "Hadn't been that Brazil come along and seen they got clear of the town without being bothered, they could've found themselves in a bad way."

"The marshal didn't just come along," Aaron Horn said, "he come a purpose."

Lockwood's thick shoulders moved slightly. "Well, whatever. What I'm getting at is this town ain't safe when them drovers are running loose and I'm saying we've got to serve notice on them to stay away."

Quite a few persons were on the street now, and several had moved up close to hear what was being said. Elsewhere along the dusty route some were out making repairs, stretching canvas over a shattered window to serve until replacement glass could be obtained, rehanging and straightening signs, re-erecting hitch racks, and such. At the far end of the street stableman Gabe McKenzie was restoring the overturned water trough to its rightful position.

"About the worst thing we could do would be to tell Cody Hungerford he can't come here with his herd no more," Avery Rankin said. "He figures this town belongs to him."

"There's some truth in the claim, too," Jergens said, "seeing as how he was the one who jawed the railroad into building the spur track. It was him that shipped the first herd out of here — and got the town started."

"If it hadn't been him it would've been me," Ben Lockwood said. "I'd been trying to get the railroad interested but never had no luck — mostly because I wouldn't fork over a lot of side money under the table."

"And he did," Gruman said. "Seems to me that sort of gives him a hold on the town."

"Not far as I'm concerned!" Lockwood snapped.

A silence fell over the men. The sun was now up and climbing, and in the steadily increasing heat they were beginning to stir restlessly. John Ashford broke the hush.

"Only one thing I can see to do and that's put it up to a vote, let everybody have a say."

"That's fair," Schulte agreed. "All should speak their mind."

"It'll have to be done right away," Brazil said. "If you vote to close the town, I'll need to post signs, head off Hungerford and anybody else coming this way."

"Voting'll be nothing but a waste of time," Lockwood said. "Anybody with good sense knows we've got to keep that trash out. Smartest thing you can do, John, is have Brazil go ahead and put up them signs, not wait."

"Pa's right," Dave Lockwood said, coming into the discussion. "Everybody'll be for it."

"Don't go betting on it!" Avery Rankin said, his voice rising. "There's quite a few that ain't here now that you can depend on being against it —"

"Meaning them saloon keepers and gamblers over in Perdition —"

"Them and some others. They've got

the right to have their say."

"Why should they?" Aaron Horn asked, shaking his head. "I don't figure they've got any right —"

"They're part of the town, even if they are on the other side of a dead line — and they're in business, same as we are," Ashford said.

"We set up that dead line," Jergens reminded, "not them. We can't cheat them out of voting."

"We won't," John Ashford said. "Pass the word along. Polls'll be open tomorrow morning, starting at seven, and the voting will go till noon. That'll give the folks living outside of town plenty of time to get in and cast their ballot. Let's be sure everybody gets the word."

7

At once the crowd began to break up, the men in singles and pairs, going on about whatever business or intentions they had in mind. Brazil, feeling the bite of hunger, went first to the Star Restaurant for an early-morning meal. Taking a chair at a table in the front of the room, he ate his plate of eggs, potatoes, and bacon, all the while listening to three men in the back, identity unknown, arguing the question of whether to close the town to the trail drivers or not.

It was going to be a tense issue, that was clear, and the outcome of the voting would be close, Brazil reckoned as he paid his check and returned to the street. There would be many broken friendships as well as heads before it was over and done with, and the scars left would be a long time healing.

Covering the short distance to his office, Luke noted that activity both for and against the proposition was apparently getting underway. A number of men, and a few women, were moving along the sidewalks, halting passersby to discuss the matter and undoubtedly attempting to persuade those who differed to their way of thought.

Ashford would have made arrangements for riders to visit the outlying residents — most likely had them already on the way — advising them of the voting that was to take place the following morning, and urging them to come in to make their wishes known. It was a subject that everyone in the area should have a voice in, and probably would. Brazil, glancing along the street at the hustling groups earnestly propounding their opinions, only hoped that it would all not get out of hand.

He reached the marshal's office, heard the noisy clamor being set up by his two prisoners, Rufe and Slim, and entered. Arkansas, corncob pipe clamped between his teeth, slumped on a bench against one of the walls, greeted him with a shake of his head.

"Them galoots you got in the poky sure are noisy fellows! Where'd they come from?"

Luke reached for the ring of keys. "Friends of that drover, Garret," he replied, and related the previous night's incidents.

Arkansas removed the pipe from his mouth, wagged his head. "Knew I should've hung around for a spell. Could've got yourself bushwhacked."

"I kept my eyes open," the lawman said, and moving on down the narrow hallway, he opened the door to the cage and released the two trail hands.

"You sure did take your time," Rufe declared sourly. "We're about starving — and we heard Parley and the rest of the boys ride out a hour ago."

"You can probably catch up with them if you hurry," Brazil said indifferently, pointing toward the front of the jail. "Find your guns laying in there on my desk. Holster them and get out of town."

"Maybe we'd as soon get us something to eat right here," Rufe said, glancing at Slim.

"Way folks out there are feeling, I'd sure not take the chance," Luke said. "And since it's me that's got to keep the peace around here, I'm ordering you not to. Fact is, if I see you anywhere around town fifteen minutes from now, you'll be right back in that cell. I make myself clear?"

Rufe mumbled an answer of some sort as he slid his weapon into the leather and stalked toward the door. Slim, nodding briskly, said, "Yes, sir" and hurriedly followed.

"Hear you had yourself a little ruckus out there in the street this morning, too," Arkansas said. "I come in sort of late to get in on it, but that hostler of Gabe McKenzie's was telling me all about it. Way I see it, folks here are stirring up a mess of trouble for themselves."

Brazil, pausing in the doorway, eyes on the two drovers just crossing the bridge over Dead Ute Creek as they hurried to retrieve their horses, turned to his desk and settled into the chair.

"We can expect plenty of it," he said. "Everything all right out at the place?"

"Everything's jake. I fed the boys and looked after the yard stock before I rode in. You figure that Sobel was aiming to take a shot at you before he pulled out?"

"Looked to me like that was what he had in mind."

"He's got the guts of a army mule — thinking he could just cut you down and then ride on! Could be the folks that're wanting to close the town down to the likes of him are right."

A yell went up in the street. Brazil glanced at Arkansas and grinned wryly. "Guess it's started," he said. Rising, he crossed to the doorway and looked out.

Down in front of Ashford's, two figures were standing toe to toe, trading blows, while a crowd of bystanders was gathering quickly.

"Who is it?" the older man asked, moving in behind the lawman.

"Rankin and Aaron Horn," Luke replied, hurrying out into the street. "Came close to mixing it up a bit earlier this morning. Had to come, I reckon."

Brazil, at a trot, made his way to where the two men, now gripping each other, blowing hard for wind, sweating freely, were wrestling back and forth. Horn, the older of the two, was getting the worst of it, that was evident. His nose was bleeding, and one eye was swelling rapidly. Rankin seemed unmarked except from effort.

Luke elbowed his way through the ring of bystanders and up to the two combatants. Grasping each by the arm, he jerked them apart.

"Back off — both of you!"

Avery Rankin pulled himself free of the lawman's fingers. "Loony old bastard!" he muttered in a low voice as he brushed at the sweat on his flushed face. "Can't talk without getting all riled up."

Horn shouted between gasps for breath: "You're wrong . . . wanting to keep . . . the town open . . . and you dang sure know it . . . only you're too dang pigheaded to admit it!"

Brazil placed his hand on the older man's shoulder, pushed him firmly toward the entrance to his store nearby, and nodded to Rankin.

"Go on back to your place, too, Avery. You're not going to settle anything this way."

Rankin shrugged and walked stiffly toward his gun-and-saddle shop. Horn had stopped, watching him.

"I sure have been wrong about him," he said heavily. "Always figured him for a friend, but I can see he ain't. It takes something like this here to open a man's eyes, that's for sure."

Arkansas, standing behind Brazil, removed his pipe and began to knock the dottle from its bowl by rapping it sharply against the heel of his hand.

"Expect Avery's thinking the same about you," he said. "Sure is a shame you two can't get together and —"

Luke turned away, stared off into the opposite direction, where a gathering had formed in front of the Palace Saloon. He recognized Ben Lockwood and Dave, along with several other townsmen. The rancher, standing on the landing of the saloon, which placed him head and shoulders above all others, was speaking rapidly and emphasizing his words with considerable gesturing.

"Old Ben's sure powerful fired up over this here thing, ain't he?" Arkansas commented as he and the lawman struck off along the roadway. "Sort of a puzzlement to me. Can't figure why he's so set on closing the town."

Brazil only shrugged. The same question had occurred to him; why was Lockwood more than ordinarily opposed to the town's continuing its role as a railhead? You would think his sympathies would lie with others like him who had need for the shipping facility.

"It's for the good of the town," Luke heard the rancher say as he and Arkansas drew up at the corner of the saloon. "Women and their young 'uns ain't safe around here no more."

"Can't see as that ought to worry you none," a voice in the crowd observed. "You don't live here — you just come in when you take the notion. Your womenfolk can stay home when them drovers are here."

"Maybe so, but that ain't the point," Lockwood shot back angrily. "I'm thinking about the women that's got homes in this town — and their kids. They have to stay here. It's them I figure we ought to be worrying about."

Arkansas nudged Luke gently. "He's mighty kindhearted all of a sudden! Don't recollect him ever before giving a hoot about anybody but hisself."

Brazil stirred, smiled. Lockwood was out of character, that was true, but he was reserving any comment. Arkansas hawked, spat.

"Ain't meaning to bad-mouth him none, Luke. I know he maybe's going to be your daddy-in-law one of these days, but I just can't help noticing —"

"Forget it," Brazil said quietly, putting a stop to the elderly man's apology. "I'm agreeing — it's not like him."

But why was Lockwood taking such a strong stand on the matter? The question, lodged in Luke's mind, would not go away. Ben had no interest in the settlement other than its being a source of supply for his ranch, which was several miles from its limits, and of course, as the railhead for shipping his beef. His contact with Moriah need be only brief and on selected occasions — why, then, was he so intensely interested in closing down the town?

Dave Lockwood had pulled away from his father and the group in the street and was entering the saloon. There was no sign of Enos Draper, who had been with the Lockwoods earlier. Likely he was busy elsewhere in the settlement, doing all he could to persuade friends and acquaintances to vote for the closing.

It could hardly be the reported bad blood between Lockwood and Cody Hungerford that was inspiring the rancher's activities. Hungerford, while being the largest cattle grower to make use of the railhead, was, after all, only one of many it served. That Lockwood would advocate turning aside all other cattlemen bringing their herds to Moriah just to spite Hungerford didn't seem reasonable.

And Luke Brazil knew that halting Cody Hungerford, should the vote go in favor of closing the town, would be no easy job. Cody was a powerful man who would brook no interference where his wishes were concerned. Most likely he would simply ignore the ban, and with the aid of his hard-case drovers, bring his herd in to the pens regardless.

Too, Hungerford would be forewarned. Parley Sobel, heading back south, would encounter Cody and pass along the word of changes on the wind in Moriah — possibly even repeating the words that Aaron Horn had shouted as he was riding out. Too, Slim and Rufe, having been present during subsequent events, would relay to Parley Sobel the news that the town was actually going to vote on whether to close itself to trail drives or not — and this also Sobel would report to Hungerford.

Luke, disturbed and dissatisfied with the way things were shaping up, began to move back toward his office. There were already more persons on the street now than there had been only minutes earlier, and he could hear voices raised in anger from several points.

"You're going to have company —"

At Arkansas's words, Brazil glanced up from his dark study. Jenny Lockwood, driving the family buggy, had swung into the street, bearing in his direction. A quiet sigh slipped from his lips. He would as soon she had remained at home, away from it all — but she had not, and there now was nothing he could do about it.

"Expect you want me hanging around, keeping a eye on things," Arkansas said half questioningly.

Brazil nodded. "I'll take it as a favor. I'm looking for plenty to be happening before the voting starts in the morning," he said resignedly, and put his attention on the girl.

8

Jenny pulled the buggy to a halt, eyes probing Brazil anxiously. When she saw that he had apparently survived the night unharmed, relief flooded her features.

"I — I hurried to town. I was afraid you might have gotten hurt," she said as he handed her down from the cushioned seat.

Brazil smiled faintly. "Don't ever waste time worrying over me. I make it a habit to look out for myself."

Jenny was frowning as she stared at the star pinned to his shirt pocket. "You're still wearing that. I thought you were going to be the marshal for only last night, until those trail drivers left town."

Brazil glanced up the street in the direction of the Palace. Ben Lockwood was still talking up the closing of the town. The crowd around him had increased considerably.

"Mayor asked me — sort of a favor — to keep it on until they could find somebody regular."

"Favor!" the girl echoed scornfully. "He has a lot of nerve to ask you for a favor after the way he — and most everybody else in this town — has treated you. You oughtn't forget that."

"I haven't," he replied, gaze shifting now to Adams' saloon, just this side of the dead line, where two men had begun to scuffle. Others were pouring out of the place, shouting, gathering to watch. Arkansas, who evidently had been inside Ashford's, on the opposite corner, was hurrying to intercede and put a stop to the fight. . . . Another disagreement on what the town should do going down to fists, Luke supposed.

"Then, why —"

"Reckon I don't blame them too much — maybe even understand them some. The kind of a man I was before I came here to settle down's not exactly the sort you'd invite to a Sunday social."

"It's not what you were — a long time ago — it's what you are now," Jenny said, brushing a straying lock of her glinting, dark hair away from a temple. "You left all that — the outlaws, the hard life with a gun — behind you. They ought to realize that."

"Not easy for some folks to forget," Brazil said.

"Well, they'd better after what you've done for them! And I wish you'd end it right now, Luke. I wish you'd take that star off, tell John Ashford to find somebody else. I don't like the thought of you going back — being what you once were and —"

"I gave the man my word," Brazil broke in quietly. "I won't go back on it."

A gunshot, coming from somewhere over beyond McKenzie's Livery Stable, echoed in the hot, still air. Luke judged the sound, gauging its distance, reckoned it was somewhere along Dead Ute Creek and well outside the town's limits.

"Papa thank you for getting mama and me out of town last evening?" Jenny asked, changing what looked to be a touchy subject.

Brazil grinned. "You expect him to?"

"Well, under the circumstances I thought he might say something."

"He did mention it while he was talking to that crowd. Probably as close as he could come to saying anything straight out."

Again Jenny brushed at her hair. "Don't let him bother you. He'll act different when the time comes for us —" Her words broke off. She looked down, then suddenly raised her head and faced him squarely. "Oh, you know what I mean!"

Luke considered the girl with a slow smile. "Been hoping you felt that way. Just never been much of a hand with words so's I could come right out and ask."

Jenny arched her dark, full brows. Mischief danced in her eyes. "Well, that's sort of a backdoor proposal, but I accept anyway. What comes next?"

Brazil rubbed at his jaw. "You mean that?"

"Of course I do!"

Luke heaved a deep sigh. "Sure glad

that much is done. You wanting to know what's next. I aim to get a decent place to live built first. Had it in mind to get it done before I did any talking about marrying."

"Have you started on it yet?"

"No. Got to sell off a few steers, get the money for lumber and such —"

"Fine," Jenny said decisively. "We can plan the house together — the arrangement, I mean. And I've got a little money of my own we can use —"

"Forget that," Brazil cut in bluntly.

"And there's the steers that I own. Papa made a habit of dividing part of the calf crop between Dave and me every spring. Did it so's we would someday have a herd of our own, he said. I suppose I have about a hundred head by now. We can sell them off —"

"Forget that, too," Luke said. "I'll get the house built and furnished on my own. You can plan how you want it — be obliged to you if you will. I've got no idea how a woman likes things fixed — but I'll do the paying."

Jenny shook her head angrily, but she

was smiling up at him. "That's nothing but pride — and you know what the Bible says about that! We could get it done much sooner if you'd let me help."

He reached out his hands, took her gently by the shoulders. "I've waited this long — another month or so's not going to hurt much." Looking about the street, he added, "No sense putting on a show for folks by standing out here. Let's get inside the jail, where it'll be sort of private. Sun's hot, anyway."

Jenny stepped up into the small office, hesitating while Brazil tied her horse to the hitch rack, and then moved deeper into the stuffy quarters when he completed the chore and followed.

"About as hot in here as it is out there in the street," he said as Jenny sank onto one of the chairs. "Best I open the back door — maybe let in a bit of a breeze."

He started for the rear of the jail, stopped, glanced toward the street as the sound of voices reached him. Coming back around, he stepped to the door and threw his glance toward the Palace. Ben Lockwood, accompanied by two dozen or so men and women, was approaching.

"What is it?" Jenny asked.

"Looks like some kind of a delegation," he answered. "Your pa's heading it up."

Jenny frowned. "Why would he —"

"Probably's got something to do with the voting tomorrow. Town's going to decide whether it wants to let the trail drives come in or not — but I reckon you already know all about it."

"I heard papa and Dave talking, but I wasn't paying them much mind. I guess that explains why there are so many people on the street, and why they seem to be arguing."

"There's a plenty of that — and there'll be more before the night's over. Folks on both sides are fired up to a fighting pitch —"

"Brazil!"

It was Ben Lockwood's voice, hard-edged and insistent. Luke stepped farther into the doorway, faced the rancher and the crowd gathered around him. Deep down, he had little use for Lockwood and his kind, but the man was Jenny's father and he would have to accept him.

"Yeh?"

"We want to know how you feel about the voting," the rancher said, the words an order rather than a request. "Folks here seem to think that since you've done a lot of knocking around the country and have run with drovers and such, you're some kind of a expert, and they want to hear what you think's best."

"We know you was a lawman," someone in the crowd explained, "and prob'ly have been up against this same thing before. You think we ought to close down the town?"

"I'm saying it ain't likely to happen again — what happened here yesterday." It was Harry Vito, the bootmaker. "I'm saying that bunch just got out of hand because we didn't have no marshal to keep the lid on them. Ain't that what you say, Brazil?"

Luke nodded slowly. "Trail hands are just men blowing off steam. They've been on the move for weeks, maybe months — and all they've seen are cows and horses and other drovers. When the drive's over and they've got cash money in their pockets they feel like celebrating — and I don't figure you ought to fault them for it."

"You mean we ought to just let them run wild?" an incredulous voice asked from the gathering.

"No, I'm saying it's the way things are and if you'll hire a good marshal and give him a couple of deputies he can —"

"Town can't afford that!" Pete Spears declared.

"You'd only need the deputies when there was a trail herd in — and then only for a couple of days. Sure ought to be able to scare up enough money for that."

There was the rumble of discussion among the crowd. Finally Ben Lockwood said, "Sounds to me like you lean towards them hell raisers."

Brazil's shoulders stirred. "Nope — and it don't mean anything to me one way or the other — but I'll tell you all this: you close this town to the drives and it'll dry up and blow away. It needs the business it gets from drovers. I've seen other towns turn their backs on the herds — and today

113

most of them are just wide places along the road."

"I can think of some that're plenty better off," Lockwood said.

"Could be, but if you'll take a close look at them I expect you'll find they had something else going for them — something to keep them alive, like a main stage-line stop, or a lot of farmers and ranchers —"

"Then you're flat out for letting the drivers come in?"

"It's neither here nor there with me. It's up to you people, who've got your money sunk in a business of some kind. I'm raising cattle, and if I can't ship them from here I'll drive them on to the next railhead.

"But if I owned a business that depended on customers I'd be for letting the trail herds come in, only I'd see that there was a good marshal with some deputy help in charge to see that the drovers stayed on the other side of the line while they were feeling their oats. That way the town would enjoy the extra cash and still not have to put up with a lot of foolishness."

"Makes sense to me," someone said quietly.

"Well, it sure'n hell don't to me!" Ben Lockwood stated flatly. "What else you expect from a man that's run with their kind all his life?" The rancher paused, glanced at the horse and buggy drawn up to the rack. "That's my rig. Brazil, is my daughter in there with you?"

The lawman glanced over his shoulder at Jenny, nodded.

"Figured as much," Lockwood said, and then, "Girl, he tell you he shot a man dead last night and then carted him over the line and dumped him in that trail boss, Sobel's, lap?"

"No, I never told her about it," Brazil said, stiffening. "No need. What's it got to do with the talk going on here?"

"Just want her to see where you really stand, that maybe you ain't put the gun behind you like she figures."

Luke again looked at Jenny. She had come to her feet, staring at him, a frown on her face.

"I was asked to take on the job of town marshal until you could find somebody to take Hurley's place. What happened last night was in the line of duty."

"That's right, Ben," Caleb Jergens said. "We can't hold what he done against him. He had to set that bunch of Sobel's down hard."

"What about Hungerford?" someone asked.

"From what I've heard, he spends a lot of money here. Let him come in — just have a lawman backed up by some good deputies set to meet him and make it plain they're to all stay on the other side of the dead line except when they're sober and wanting to do business. I'd see that they checked their guns, too, was I the marshal."

"Cody Hungerford'd never listen to that kind of hogwash!" Lockwood said in disgust.

"I expect he would. He needs this railhead. It shaves a couple of weeks off a drive that he'd have to make if it wasn't here and he had to go on to Trinity Crossing. I doubt if he's one to spite himself."

"You don't know him!" Lockwood

said. "He'd cut his own throat if it'd help him get his way about something."

Brazil shrugged. "Seems you do — all a lot of wasted talking, anyway. People are going to vote in the morning, decide whether they're going to let him or anybody else bring a herd into here. Have to see first which way it's to be, then make plans."

"And your advice is to keep the town open?" Jergens pressed.

"Long as you get yourself a good marshal and give him a couple of deputies — yes."

"Well, I ain't agreeing with that — and I reckon the town won't either!" Ben Lockwood said, brushing at the sweat shining on his broad face. "And that's how all decent folks around here'll see it."

Abruptly the rancher wheeled, and angrily pushing his way through the crowd, headed for the Palace Saloon. It was evident to Luke that the rancher had been expecting support from him for his position to close down Moriah and was furious when he didn't get it. He reckoned he'd widened the chasm between Jenny's father and himself even farther.

The lawman remained in the doorway, hearing the approving comments of some gathered in front of the jail, the contrary opinions of others as they began to disperse. But they'd asked — and he'd spoken his mind, told them truthfully what he thought.

"You — you can't mean what you said —"

Frowning, Brazil came about. Jenny, hands clenched into tiny fists, was facing him. In the reflected light from the street the blue of her eyes was very bright.

"Told them how I saw it — and how it ought to be far as I was concerned," he said, and watched despair claim her features.

"It was a mistake — letting John Ashford talk you into being the marshal," Jenny murmured in a lost sort of voice. "It can only start you thinking and remembering the kind of life you used to lead — and maybe wishing you could go back."

Luke Brazil tossed his hat onto the desk, leaned up against the wall. Folding his arms across his chest, he studied her.

"No, not likely."

She had been looking off into the street. Abruptly she faced him. There was the hint of tears in her eyes. "You can't deny it, Luke! I saw it in you yesterday when you came to help mama and me. You enjoy being a lawman — using a gun — fighting — all the excitement!"

"It was a way to make a living — once." Brazil said quietly. "Nothing wrong with that, is there?"

"A lot!" Jenny cried. "The people you were around, associated with — the outlaws and killers — and renegades and trail hands like the men that were just here — they were bound to rub off on you some, cause you to look at things in the same light they do."

Luke digested that slowly. From the street came the sound of men running — the pound of boot heels, shouts, the excited barking of a dog. Another difference of opinion on the voting being settled with fists, he guessed.

A faint stir of anger was beginning to move him. It seemed to him Jenny was being unreasonable, but he kept his tone low and at a normal level.

"And you used your gun — killed a man, and then made a show of it," she continued.

"Sometimes it's necessary. When you're dealing with a bunch of hard cases it's smart to let them see that you're tougher than they are — or make them think it." He paused as the anger within him heightened. "What did you expect me to do — stand there and let myself get shot? I was the marshal —"

"You said you'd never again use a gun on a man —"

"Recollect saying I hoped I'd never need to —"

"It's the same —"

Brazil was of a mind to argue the point, but he let it drop. Jenny was distraught, was working herself up to an even greater pitch.

"This kind of talk's crazy," he said gently. "We're blowing up a storm over nothing —"

"Do you call taking sides with those drovers — against papa and the merchants — nothing?"

"I was asked what I thought the town ought to do — my opinion. I gave it. Happens your pa didn't agree."

"But you're favoring the drovers over the decent people of the town!"

"No such thing!" he said sharply, patience beginning to ebb. "The town can't afford to lose the cash business that trail drives bring in —"

"Moriah's better off without that kind of business."

"Maybe, but that doesn't change the fact that it still needs it. There'll be a lot of folks get hurt if the drives quit coming here — people who've sunk their lives into a store and —"

"There are still the ranchers and the homesteaders and the ones who live here."

"Not enough of them to keep a whole town going. Takes cash coming in from the outside."

"Saloon money — that's the only kind trail drives bring in!" Jenny's voice rose almost to a shout. "Money that's spent on whiskey and gambling and — and those women!"

"Still good, hard cash that ends up finally in the pockets of the merchants right along this street. And not all drovers blow their wages in Perdition, anyway. There's plenty of them come over and buy themselves new saddles and boots and clothes — maybe even treat themselves to a new gun."

Brazil fell silent. Jenny was shaking her head slowly. "You see, you're taking their side, defending them, trying to make them look like —"

"No such thing!" Luke said bluntly, anger at last coming to the surface and again sharpening his tone. "I'm just facing the truth. Not everybody in this world is the Sunday-go-to-meeting sort. There's a plenty of the tough, hard-case kind too, and you learn to live with them. It'd be fine if we could turn our backs and they'd go away — but they won't, so we've got no choice other'n to make the best of it."

"Are you saying we should associate with them?"

"No!" Brazil replied wearily. "It'll be a mite hard for somebody like you, who's had most everything, to understand, but there are a lot of people around that are struggling to survive. They try to get along with everybody, regardless of who or what they are."

Jenny had moved close to the window and was gazing out into the street. The sidewalks were fairly well crowded despite the rising heat, and it was evident the people of Moriah were taking the matter of closing the settlement to the trail drives very seriously.

"Is money so important to you, Luke?"

Surprised by the question, and failing to see its relevance, he shrugged, brushed at the sweat on his forehead. "Don't know what that's got to do with you and me, but I figure it's just something to make use of. Far as the town closing the trail or leaving it open, it won't matter to me. I don't have a stake in any business to look out for."

"Then, I can't see why you'd take such a strong stand — against my father and the people who want to keep the bad element out of town —"

"We're going around in circles!" Luke broke in, anger once more edging his tone.

"I've made it clear I think it's best for the town."

"Even if it means letting a man like Cody Hungerford and his wild bunch come in — take over?"

"I doubt if he and his crew are any worse than Parley Sobel and his crowd — or a few others. Goes right back to having a lawman with enough help to keep the peace."

"But you can't be sure a marshal can control Cody Hungerford. I heard papa say that —"

"Whatever it is between him and Hungerford shouldn't have anything to do with what's best for the town. You know that, Jenny. It's something personal — goes way back, I'm told — and I think your pa's against Hungerford because of that, not because he's worrying about the town."

"You can't say that!" Jenny flared, whirling to face him.

"That's sure how it looks to me — and I expect some others around here. Why else would it make any difference to him?"

"He's thinking of mama and me —

other women —"

"Far as you and your mother are concerned, you can stay clear of here when there's drovers in town. You don't have to come in."

"But I have that right —"

"Sure. I expect women in other railhead towns have told themselves the same thing, only if they were thinking about the people who depended on the trail hands for a livelihood, they avoided trouble by keeping off the streets."

Jenny tossed her head angrily. "Well, papa won't let me look at it that way! He thinks we should be able to go where we please and not be afraid — that the streets have to be safe all the time — not just part — for everybody."

"He tell you that?"

Jenny frowned, stared at him. "Are you doubting my word, Luke?"

"No, of course not. But I'm wondering when he said something like that. Was it today, last night maybe, or was it a long time ago?"

"Oh, I don't know — and I can't see that it matters. What does is that this whole thing has come between us right when I thought we —"

He turned to her as her voice broke, took her in his arms. "We're fools to let this — or anything — come between us," he said, his manner softening.

"Then, why can't you see my side of it?"

He stiffened slightly. "You mean your pa's side. I don't think you'd given it a thought when you drove in. It was only after he and that crowd came here, asked me how I felt about it, that you started feeling the way you do."

Jenny pulled herself away from him, moved toward the door. She was suddenly rigid, her manner icy cold and distant.

"It doesn't really matter," she murmured, and stepped out into the open.

"Wait — Jenny —" Brazil called, taking a hurried stride after her.

"Never mind," she replied with a shake of her head, and freeing the rope from the bar of the hitch rack, she looped it into the mare's halter and climbed into the buggy. Prim, shoulders stiff, head high, she drove off down the street.

9

"She's got the vapors," Dave Lockwood said.

The evening meal was over, and he was with his mother, father, and sister on the broad veranda of the ranch house, soaking in the welcome coolness that was settling over the land. Down at the cookshack the cook was whistling cheerfully, as if glad the long day was finally coming to an end. Most of the crew — those not assigned to nighthawk — had already cleaned up after their stint on the range and had ridden into town.

May Lockwood, hands folded in her lap, lovely features set to soft lines, wide, blue eyes calm, smiled at her daughter.

"What is it, Jenny?"

The girl, sitting in a rocker near the end of the porch, gaze lost on the ragged rim of the Skulls etched against the sky, only shrugged.

"Had a spat with Luke Brazil — that's what," Dave said, grinning broadly. "Friend of mine happened to be passing the jail, heard them going at it."

Jenny turned, favoring her brother with a cold look. She had long ago accepted the fact that she could never match the outstanding, if passive, beauty of her mother, had compensated for the lack by developing a strong personality.

"I'll be obliged to you if you'll mind your own business," she said in a withering tone.

"Brazil is our business," Ben Lockwood said, speaking the words slowly, distinctly as he flicked the ashes from the tip of his cigar. "Made himself clear on where he stands — flat out against me. I want you staying away from him, girl."

Jenny came up out of her chair slowly. Her full, well-shaped lips were no more than a tight line.

"Don't give me orders, Papa —"

"As long as you're living under my roof you'll do what I tell you, and I'm —"

"We've been through this before," Jenny said quietly. "All you need to do is say the word and I'll move into town — into Mrs. Haskell's Boardinghouse."

May Lockwood sighed deeply. Ben clenched the cigar between his teeth. He had never been able to cope with his daughter and her stubborn sense of independence, not even when she was a child. Jenny was like him; it pleased him to think that, but he wished it had been the other way around insofar as his offspring were concerned; instead, Dave was inclined to be like his mother — and a son should take after his father.

"Brazil's against me," the rancher said, sidestepping the challenge Jenny had laid down. "And that's the same as being against the family. His name goes down on my black list along with a few other so-called friends I talked to this morning."

"Black list?" Mrs. Lockwood echoed, mustering a frown.

"That's what I said. Far as I'm concerned, a man is either with me all the way or he's against me. There ain't no middle ground — which brings me up to you, Dave —"

"Yeh, Pa?"

"I want you to ride into town tonight, rustle around and do some listening. I need to know how things are shaping up — and who all's going to be voting for closing the town and who's not."

"Yes, sir."

"I expect you to do some talking, too. Anybody you run into who's for letting the herds come in, try changing their mind. Don't be scared to speak up. The Lockwood name carries a lot of weight, and now's the time to make use of it. Now, if you feel the need to buy a few rounds of drinks go ahead — stand the crowd if you like. It's good politicking. Tell Gruman or Joe Adams, or wherever you happen to be, that I said it was all right and I'll settle with them when I come in tomorrow."

Dave had risen to his feet. "I savvy, Pa. You can leave it to me."

"You'll be running into some of our crew. Tell them I want them doing the same thing — only, forget about them

130

buying whiskey on me. They can pay for their own."

"Sure thing," Dave said, his pleasure at being entrusted with a task so significant sparkling in his eyes. Lithe, dark, but without the firm, set features, he was in appearance a younger edition of his father.

"Ben," Mrs. Lockwood said hesitantly, "I — I'm not sure you should let —"

"He'll be all right, May," Lockwood assured her, studying the glowing tip of his cigar. He would have felt better and more confident if it were Jenny he was sending in, but a man didn't send his daughter on such an errand.

"About time he took a part in running things, anyway," the rancher continued gruffly. "This'll give him a good chance to see what persuading folks to do what he wants is like."

"You won't be gone too long, will you?" the older woman asked, reaching a slim hand to her son. "No later than midnight —"

"He'll be home when he figures it's time," Ben said, drawing back her arm.

131

"If he's going to be the man I expect him to, we've got to let him go on his own — and without any of your damned apron strings dragging at him. . . . Have a care, son."

"Sure, Pa, I will," Dave replied happily, and pivoting, stepped down off the porch and headed for the corral at a fast walk.

For a few moments Ben Lockwood watched his son move off into the warm, mellow darkness and then turned his attention to Jenny.

"We were talking about Brazil," he began, his voice low, manner chary. "Some things we need to hash over —"

Jenny smiled tightly, rose, and started for the door. "If it's to be about Luke, Papa, save your breath. It's all over between us, I expect."

Lockwood sat up hurriedly. Removing the cigar from between his teeth, he stroked his mustache in a quick, satisfied way, and smiled.

"I knew you'd come to your senses! I tried to tell you before that he wasn't our kind — that he was no good for you."

Jenny paused, looked back at her parent.

"I wonder, Papa. After thinking over today I'm about of the opinion that I'm not good enough for *him*. . . . See you all in the morning."

Ben Lockwood swore softly under his breath as the door closed behind his daughter. There was no understanding the girl.

10

The day passed quickly for Luke Brazil, giving him little time to think about the misunderstanding that had risen like a wall between Jenny Lockwood and himself.

There had been numerous meetings in the settlement, some organized by those supporting the closing of the town, others called by the ones opposed. The latter forces were now being aided by several residents and property owners from across the dead line, in Perdition, where the discontinuance of the trail-herd business would mean certain bankruptcy, should it come to pass.

Led by Jed Tillman, all concerned were throwing themselves wholeheartedly into the campaign. That their assistance was not being enthusiastically welcomed by many south of the line was of no consequence to them; they wanted only to keep the drovers coming.

Near dark, after finally agreeing with Arkansas that they would cease all efforts to prevent or halt the fights that broke out periodically along the street as long as no weapons were involved, Luke treated himself to supper at the Star and then returned to his office.

There, dragging one of the chairs out onto the small landing that fronted the building, he cocked the piece of straight-backed furniture against the wall and settled down. He was tired, humorless, and wishing it was all over with, but the worst, he suspected, was yet to come.

From the way it looked at the moment, it appeared the faction desiring to keep Moriah open to the trail drives had the most support — but their opponents were far from giving up.

Luke had noticed hired hands from Lockwood's, Draper's, and two of the other ranches, all freshly shaven and wearing clean shirts, circulating about the town. Most likely dispatched by Ben Lockwood and the ranchers siding with him, they no doubt had been instructed to do all they possibly could for the cause. Later, Brazil saw young Dave Lockwood ride in, probably to add his efforts to those of the ranch hands.

Again Brazil wondered why the closing of the trail was so important to Ben Lockwood, and once more found himself at a loss for a logical answer. He was certain the rancher was not all that public-spirited — so much so he'd go to such lengths to keep out the drovers for the sake of Moriah, as he professed; Lockwood had never been known to take so great an interest in the welfare of the settlement before — why now?

Luke's attention swung to the hunched shape of Arkansas advancing toward him in the increasing darkness.

"Needing a mite of help," the old man said, producing his pipe as he dropped to his heels beside Luke. "Folks are ranting about that bunch from Perdition being over here, talking up keeping the trail open."

"Can't keep them from doing that," Brazil said.

"Just what I told them. They're worrying about the voting, come tomorrow. Claim Jed and them ain't got the right."

"If they own property over there, they have. Perdition is still a part of the town. Who all's there?"

Arkansas lit his pipe, puffed at it for a moment. "Well, besides Tillman there's Long John Green and Sam Hester, and that restaurant fellow, Steele, and Art Hurd — and Melly Jones."

Brazil, eyes on a crowd in front of the Palace Saloon, nodded. All mentioned were in business — even Melly Jones, who owned and operated the bawdyhouse on the far side of the cattle pens.

"They've got a right to a vote, far as I know," he said. "We can let Ashford pass on it in the morning."

"Then, it's all right for them to be talking up their side of it?"

"Let them have at it. Nothing wrong."

"What about their hired help?"

Brazil shook his head, attention again on his old friend. "Best they keep out of it — 'specially any of Melly's girls. Can't cause anything but trouble if they're running loose on the street."

"They're supposed to stay on the other side of the line, anyway."

"That's the rule, only I think Hurley's been letting them come over, do some buying when there's no drovers around. Jed Tillman and the others'll be smart to keep them out of it. Folks see a bunch of doxies roaming about could cause them to maybe change their mind and vote to close the trail . . . How you like being a deputy?"

"Fine, fine," Arkansas replied, rising. "Sort of reminds me of the time we was down in that there little town on the Mex border — over in Arizona. Wasn't no regular deputy then, but I sure was having me some fun traipsing around after you."

"We've been a few places together, all right," Brazil said, "and some of them weren't exactly healthy. If you get tired and want to catch a few winks, let me know."

"I'll do it. You going to be here for a spell?"

"Only for a few more minutes. Aim to

start making the rounds again. Looks like we'll be doing that for the rest of the night.''

"For certain," Arkansas said and moved off down the street.

Luke watched the older man disappear into the shadows. Night had all but claimed the settlement now, and lamps were being lit in the stores and houses. The church sexton, whose job it was to light the half dozen street lamps, bought and erected by public subscription, had not yet put in his appearance, but that was not unusual. He customarily waited until full dark before touching a match to the wicks of the metal-and-glass squares atop poles placed variously along the route.

There appeared to be something more extensive than an ordinary argument taking place in front of Joe Adams' saloon, at the end of the block, and coming to his feet, Brazil made his way leisurely through the cooling but dust-filled air toward that point.

As he drew near, he recognized Adams, a squat, white-haired man with black brows and spade beard, standing on a whiskey keg in front of his saloon haranguing a group of men and women who had paused to listen. Adams looked to be fairly well liquored up, which was unusual, as he was known to be an abstainer.

"We can't let them blue-nose holy Joes ruin this here town of our'n!" he was shouting as Luke halted along the fringe of the crowd. "There's a many of us that's got every last dime we own sunk in what we're doing. It ain't right to have it took away from us by them that ain't got nothing to lose!"

"If you're aiming that at my pa, you're a damn liar!" Dave Lockwood yelled back, stepping up onto the landing near the saloon man. "He's got as much to lose as anybody else!"

"How can your pa lose?" Adams demanded. "He ain't running no business to go bust when there ain't nobody coming in and buying. All him and them other cattlemen've got to worry about is getting their steers to the market, and that ain't no sweat. Way I see it, the ranchers hadn't ought to get to vote on this — only the folks that're in business and stand to lose out."

Shouts of agreement went up from the gathering. "Somebody ought to talk to the mayor about that!" a voice declared.

"Hell, they got as much right to have a say as anybody else," another bystander countered.

"Not the way I figure —"

Brazil turned, headed back up the street as there was sudden commotion somewhere on the far side of the crowd. Another fight. Let them settle it between themselves. The argument was pointless, anyway; Lockwood and the ranchers, powerful factors in the area, would get their vote.

Moving slowly along the roadway, now alight from the gleam of the street lamps, Luke probed the stores, the passageways, and the shadowy corners carefully as he passed, searching for any suspicious activity.

People along the way nodded or spoke, some pleasantly, others in a not so friendly fashion. But he was giving little thought to them, or to the job he was performing; he found his mind reverting to the minutes, earlier that day, when he and Jenny

Lockwood had come to a parting. Several times since it had occurred, the remembrance of it had sought to occupy him, but being a man of single purpose, he had kept to the continuous string of problems with which he was faced, and had thrust the matter, however personally important, aside. Now it was different; deciding to ignore the noisy quarrels and fisticuffs left him more or less to himself and on his own — and there was time to think.

Just how it had all come about was still unclear to him. At the beginning it had been an easy, agreeable conversation pertaining to what awaited them, and then Ben Lockwood had appeared with a number of the townspeople in tow and everything had changed.

He had simply spoken what he believed to be right, and in those few words he'd uttered, a curtain of ice had seemed to descend and close him off from Jenny. He'd tried to surmount it but said all the wrong things, it now appeared, and, shortly after, she was gone, making it clear that all that had existed between them was over. How the hell could it be? How could anything so fine, so strong as the feeling between them end so fast? If that was all there was to —

The flat crack of a pistol brought Luke Brazil around. The shot had come from the direction of Joe Adams'. The gathering he'd witnessed a short time earlier had broken up, and there were now only three or four persons to be seen.

"Marshal . . . get the marshal . . . somebody!"

A man had appeared suddenly on the landing of the saloon. Immediately, Brazil started for the lower end of the street at a brisk run. Someone had resorted to his gun as a means of settling an argument. Throughout the day, Luke had feared it would happen — and now it had.

When he drew abreast of Vito's Shoe & Boot Shop, Brazil slowed, eyes catching sight of a man spurting from the rear door of Adams' place and rushing off into the blackness beyond. The hurrying figure, moving through the shaft of light coming from a back window of the building, had been clearly visible.

"Marshal," the man waiting on the landing called as he caught sight of the lawman's approach. "Joe Adams's been shot — dead."

Luke didn't need to wait for the succeeding words; he knew beforehand what they would be.

"Dave Lockwood did it! Just pulled his pistol and started shooting — and Joe wasn't even armed!" Brazil, face taut, reached the saloon and crossing its landing, entered the dimly lit, smoke-filled room. The smell of gun-powder, mixing with the odors of sweat, stale beer, and whiskey hung heavily in the not-large area, and the quick run of talk ended abruptly at his appearance.

A dozen or more patrons were on hand, and all were gathered at the moment around the saloon man, lying on the sawdust-covered floor in front of the bar. A dark stain on his chest marked the entrance of the bullet.

"How'd it happen?" Luke asked, crouching beside the body and feeling for a pulse. He was confident there was no life remaining in Adams, but he had to be sure.

"Him and Ben Lockwood's boy was arguing something fierce," Jake, Adams' bartender, said, coming out from behind the counter. "They was both plenty sore."

"Heard Joe tell the boy to get out," a man standing nearby volunteered. "It riled Joe to have that kid in here talking up closing the trail while he was doing all he could to keep it open and stay in business."

"That when the shooting started?" Brazil asked. He had found no pulse, and was now checking the saloon man's body for a weapon. There was none.

"Right about. The boy wouldn't go, so Joe grabbed him by the arm, started to throw him out. That's when it happened."

"No gun on Adams. Anybody see one?"

"He weren't carrying none, Marshal," Jake said. "Joe hardly ever did."

"I don't think Lockwood's boy knew that," the man near the bar said. "Expect he just figured Joe had a pistol. He ain't no murderer."

"You're wrong, Harley," Jake said, pointing at the saloon man's body. "Joe laying there proves it. Now, I'm for getting a bunch together and going out after him!"

"You'll stay right here tending bar," Brazil said coldly. "That goes for everybody else. I'll take care of Dave Lockwood."

"That mean you're going to arrest him — hold him for murder?"

Luke nodded. A thread of bitterness ran through him. Why did it have to be Dave Lockwood — Jenny's brother? Why couldn't it have been someone else? Matters were bad enough with her already — and now, having to go after Dave —

"That'll be the charge," he said. "Soon as this voting's over I'll get a judge in here for a trial."

"You can figure on plenty of witnesses," the bartender said. "Everybody in here seen the kid do it — seen him shoot Joe down cold-blooded as you please. That boy's got to hang."

"That's for damn sure," someone in the crowd added. "But I ain't so sure we're smart in waiting for some judge to show up that Ben Lockwood'll probably buy off before it's over with. Could be, waiting'll be a waste of time."

"Maybe so," Luke said, pulling back to where he had a broader view of the crowd, now increased somewhat by passersby on the street hearing the shouting and entering to see what it was all about. "But that's the way it's going to be. Anybody with other ideas about taking matters into his own hands will have to go through me."

There was a long breath of silence, and then a voice deep in the gathering said: "You ain't aiming to favor him none because he's your lady friend's brother, are you, Marshal?"

"He'll get treated the same as anybody else, no better nor worse," Brazil replied coolly. "Some of you carry Adams up to Ed Feeney's. Go by the alley. I'd just as soon this wouldn't get around just yet."

"You going to try to keep it quiet?" Jake asked, rubbing at his jaw.

Luke glanced over the crowd with a sardonic eye. "Not much chance of that, I reckon," he said. "Just like to have Dave in a cell by the time the rest of the town knows about it."

The   bartender   muttered   his

understanding. "You going after him now?"

Brazil said, "That's what I've got in mind," and pivoting, headed for the door. He slowed as several men moved to follow. "I won't be needing any help," he added quietly, motioning them back. "Just go on about your business."

He waited until all had turned away, and then walked on, pushing open the screen door, which Joe Adams had preferred to the usual swinging batwings, stepping out onto the landing and down into the street.

Men were still hurrying up, shouting back and forth, asking questions as they came. Luke caught a glimpse of Arkansas farther along. The old man was approaching at a limping trot. Brazil, throwing a glance to the rear of the saloon, where he had last seen Dave, halted.

"Hear Ben Lockwood's boy shot down Joe Adams!"

Luke swore. He might as well forget his hope to get Dave behind bars before word of the killing became general knowledge.

"Sure got around fast —"

Arkansas spat, wiped at his mouth with

the back of a wrist. "It was that jackass Coalie Parsons. Come busting into the Palace a yelling it at the top of his voice. I shut him up plenty quick, but he'd done told everybody along the street. It for sure Joe's dead?"

Luke pointed toward the rear of the saloon. Several men, carrying Adams between them, had emerged and were starting up the alley for Feeney's.

"Too bad," Arkansas said. "Can't say that Joe was no great shakes as a man, but he didn't deserve killing. Any doubt who done it?"

"No. I saw Dave come running out the back when I came up. And there's about a dozen men that witnessed it."

"I reckon they was arguing over closing the town."

"That's what it was all about. Bad part of it is that Adams wasn't carrying a gun."

The older man whistled softly. "Going to go hard on the boy, that's for sure."

"Be worse if a lynch mob gets started. I stopped the talk of one back there in the saloon a bit ago, but if the word's all over town we could be in real trouble."

Arkansas, eyes on a crowd in front of the Antlers, nodded. "You can say that again. You got a hunch where he is?"

"No," Brazil said. "I saw him come out of the saloon and head off into the dark. I watched him ride in earlier and leave his horse out back of the Palace. He would've been going after it if he aimed to get out of town."

"Just about what he done."

"I'm not too sure. I don't think Ben Lockwood figured on Dave doing any shooting. Boy won't want to face up to him."

"Maybe not, but don't go forgetting Dave's old Ben's son and the boy'll look to him for help — which he sure'n hell will get. What are you planning on doing?"

"I'd like for you to keep on walking the street, try to keep the lid on things. I'm going to have a look around for Dave. Good chance he's scared and's hiding out somewhere in town —"

"What if he ain't?"

"Then, he'll most likely be at the

Lockwood ranch, and I'll go out there."

Arkansas considered that in silence. Then, scratching at his jaw, he said, "Maybe I best be doing that, knowing how things are between you and the Lockwoods."

A yell went up from the group in front of the hotel as something was said by someone that met with approval. Brazil stirred.

"I'm obliged to you, Arky, but it's my job. Won't make much difference now, anyway."

The older man clucked sympathetically. "It all that bad, eh? Heard talk, didn't put no stock in it. I'm real sorry about it. . . . I'll keep my eye peeled for the boy too. Like you say, he's either here or out at the Box B. If'n I turn him up, I'll throw him in the calaboose quick, before anybody knows about it, and get word to you."

Brazil nodded and moved off into the darkness beyond the street. He heard Arkansas's passing comments to people along the way, cheerful and friendly, but within himself there was no feeling of affability as he began the search for Dave Lockwood; there was only a sense of heaviness.

Two hours later, after having made as thorough a probe of the settlement as possible, under the circumstances, for the boy and finding no trace of him, Luke Brazil resigned himself to the inevitable; he had no choice except to go to the Lockwood ranch and arrest Dave, for there, undoubtedly, was where he was hiding.

Such meant bracing Ben Lockwood, who certainly would not surrender his son without a fight. That, however, was of small consequence; it was the thought of facing Jenny, seeing the hurt, the accusation in her eyes, that he disliked.

11

The windows of the Box B ranch house were rectangles of yellow light when Brazil rode into the yard, well after midnight. Other structures — the bunkhouse, the barn, the cookshack, and such lesser buildings — were totally dark, as he could expect them to be at that hour.

Grim, Luke pulled up to the hitch rack in the yard fronting the long, rambling structure. He sat for a few moments listening to the faraway yapping of a coyote, and then, dismounting, wrapped the reins of his bay horse around the crossbar, stepped up onto the full-width porch, and knocked on the door.

There was no immediate response. Brazil half turned, let his eyes run the neatly kept yard with its whitewashed rock border, its beds of bright-colored flowers

153

clearly visible in the moonlight. The heavy scent of lilacs hung in the warm, still air, and over in the small orchard of fruit trees to his left a mockingbird was singing.

This is how it could have been for me, he thought disconsolately, *the kind of peace and beauty a man dreams of and works for, or perhaps will even kill for.* But it was not for him; he'd missed his chance and it was unlikely, after the minutes that lay ahead for him, it would ever come again.

Shoulders down, he came back around, again rapped on the thick panel. Once more there was silence, and then abruptly the heavy door swung inward and Ben Lockwood, pistol in hand, stood before him.

"What the hell you want?" the rancher demanded.

Beyond Lockwood's towering bulk Luke could see Jenny and her mother standing in the center of the room that served as the parlor. Both were wearing night clothes. Lockwood had pulled on pants and jacket.

"You know what I want," Brazil said quietly.

The rancher's face darkened angrily. "I know you best be getting out of here — coming in the middle of the night, waking folks up —"

The lawman shook his head. "No use trying to fool each other, Ben. I saw light in your windows for more'n a mile off. You've been up and around for hours — and we both know why."

May Lockwood began to weep brokenly. Jenny, speaking softly, placed an arm about her mother as she sought to comfort her.

"He ain't here," Lockwood said abruptly, evidently concluding there was little point in feigning ignorance. "Don't know where he went."

Brazil studied the rancher's strained features. "I'll have to look around, Ben —"

"You can take my father's word for it," Jenny said coolly, stepping forward. "He's not a liar."

Luke shifted his attention to the girl. Her eyes looked darker, deep-set, and showed signs of weeping. He felt a knife twist inside him as he realized the vastness of the gulf that now lay between them.

"I know that, but I'll have to do it anyway. It's my job."

"Your job!" Jenny cried. "It's not your job — you're just making it so! Everything would be all right for us if you hadn't taken it in your head to wear a gun — be a lawman again!"

"I never asked for it," Brazil replied doggedly.

He could have explained that he had been of a mind to turn down John Ashford's plea to assume the marshal's job until told that she and her mother were in danger. But now it would sound like a weak excuse and his pride would not let him make use of it, even if true.

"Now you can see what it has brought to us!" Jenny continued, her voice ragged with sobs. "You're here after my brother — and you'll likely — likely kill him too!"

"No, not if I can keep from it."

"But you will — I just know! And after you've done it you'll tell yourself it was your duty!"

It was Mrs. Lockwood comforting Jenny now. She had put aside her own tears, had stepped in next to the distraught girl and taken her into her arms.

Brazil shrugged wearily, glanced at Lockwood, standing silent through the outburst. "Where is he, Ben? The best thing he can do is come with me. There's already lynch talk. I've stopped it so far, but unless Dave comes along with me, lets me lock him up—"

"Lynch!" Lockwood exclaimed, as if suddenly realizing what the lawman had said. "By God, if any of them hay shakers and counterjumpers want more trouble than they ever thought of, let them start something like that!"

"Good chance they'll try. Joe Adams wasn't packing a gun when Dave shot him. That's got feeling running pretty high — but I figure I can keep things in hand if I've got Dave locked up by morning."

"They'll try taking him away from you if it's all that bad —"

"Try — but it'll end there. You've got my word on that."

"Hell, your word ain't going to stop no

lynch mob!'' the rancher shouted. ''And that there cracker box of a jail —''

''If worse comes to worst I'll move him, but I don't figure that will ever be necessary. People around here are all fired up over voting on whether the town's going to be closed or not. That'll keep their minds off Dave. Meantime I'll send word out for the judge to come in, hold a trial — and bring along some deputies if we need them.''

''What chance has that boy got?'' Lockwood said, his manner softening, becoming almost pleading. ''And that's all he is — a boy. Just lost his head.''

''I know that, and some of the men who saw it happen are saying they don't think Dave knew Joe Adams was unarmed.''

''He didn't. He told me he figured Adams was reaching for his iron when he threw down on him.''

''Could be the way it was. It'll come out in a trial. Now, where is he, Ben? Only smart thing for you to do is let me take him in and put him in a cell, where he'll be safe.''

The rancher's attitude underwent change

once more. His features hardened, and a belligerence came into his eyes.

"I ain't buying that, Brazil! He's safer right here with me and my boys — and I've got enough of them to hold off any damned posse or lynch mob that comes out here looking for him!

"And far as letting him stand trial around here, I ain't going for that either. Down deep, most of them townspeople hate my guts. Hate Dave too, because he's a Lockwood. Any jury made up of them'll put a rope around his neck for sure! No, you plain, flat forget it. I ain't turning my son over to you so's he can get hung for killing a no-account like Joe Adams. . . . Now, I'm ordering you off my property!"

"No, Papa, let him have his look around," Jenny said, her composure regained. "He's the law. Let him see for himself that Dave's not here — that we're not hiding him in the house."

The rancher frowned. He slid a glance at his daughter from the corner of an eye, scrubbed at his jaw. "I ain't no hand to let strangers go poking around —"

"He's the marshal," Jenny said.

"We've got to let him do his job. He can start looking right here in this room, then I'll take him through the rest of the house."

Brazil brushed aside the anger Jenny's sneering tone evoked. "I doubt if he's in here," he said dryly, and wheeling, started back across the porch.

"Where you think you're going?" Lockwood asked hastily.

"Bunkhouse," the lawman replied. "And if I don't find him there I'll keep right on hunting until —"

The sudden pound of hoofs somewhere beyond the crew's quarters brought Luke Brazil up short. A curse slipped from his lips. While he'd been wasting time talking to Jenny and her father, Dave had been making his escape. Pivoting, Luke crossed to his horse and, jerking the reins free, vaulted into the saddle. Throwing a glance at the Lockwoods, now out on the veranda, he nodded curtly.

"I'm obliged to you for nothing — and I sure hope you don't end up being sorry for what you've done," he said and spurred off into the shadows.

Circling the house, he started across the yard. Dave was apparently heading for the Skulls, but just what area of the long, trailing range it would be impossible to tell — unless he could catch up with the boy enough to see which direction he was taking.

A half dozen dark figures suddenly rose up in the darkness ahead of Brazil. Shouting, waving hats, jackets, even a blanket, they presented a noisy, frightening barrier to the horse the lawman was riding. The big gelding veered, went up on his hind legs, started to fall. Brazil kicked free of the stirrups, threw himself clear of the flailing hoofs of the struggling horse, and went sprawling onto the dusty hardpack.

Furious, slightly stunned from the blow his head had taken as he struck the ground, Luke pulled himself upright. Nearby, the gelding was scrambling to his feet, shaking himself as he again was solidly on four legs.

The lawman touched the butt of his pistol, assured himself the weapon had not fallen from the holster when he went

161

down, and laid his cold attention on the line of cowhands watching him silently. They had succeeded in preventing him from following Dave, and determining now which end of the mountains he'd struck for was out of the question. The boy could have gone north, south, or borne straight into the heart of the ragged formation.

There was nothing he could do now but call in Arkansas to track Dave — and that would have to wait until daylight. Stepping back, he moved toward the waiting bay; he might as well spend the remainder of the night in town. Immediately, several of the Box B cowhands moved forward to block him.

"Reckon you'd best wait till Mister Lockwood says you can go," one drawled.

Brazil slowed, came up stiffly. His tall, straight shape poised threateningly, he faced the man in the strong moonlight.

"Get the hell out of my way," he said in a voice pulsing with anger.

The rider hesitated, glanced uncertainly about, but he did not give ground. "Mister Lockwood said —"

"I don't give a goddam what Lockwood said!" Brazil snarled, and dropped his hand onto the pistol at his side. "If you don't want more trouble than you can swallow, keep out of my way!"

Ignoring the men, Luke stepped up to his horse. Swinging onto the saddle, he cut the big gelding, still trembling from his fall, about.

"Play it smart," he warned the silently watching hired hands softly. "I'm passing over what you done. Next time, it'll be different."

12

First light had faded, and a rose-tinted dawn was filling the eastern sky when Brazil reached Moriah. Quite a number of persons were abroad at that early hour, many, he suspected, probably never having gone home, waiting out the night so as to be on hand early for the voting.

Luke rode the half length of the street to his office and, picketing the bay at the rack, entered. Arkansas was dozing on a cot in one of the cells.

"Just grabbing myself a bit of shut-eye," the older man said, coming to his feet at the thud of Brazil's boot heels. "Where's the boy?"

"Got by me and headed into the Skulls," Brazil said. "I came for you. We'll have to track him —"

"Best you do some talking to the mayor

first. He come looking for you last night after you'd lit out for the Lockwood place. Said you and me was to keep an eye on the voting. Seems he's figuring on there being trouble."

Brazil clawed at the shadow of dark whiskers on his jaw. "He know about Dave?"

"Reckon so —"

Abruptly Luke wheeled, started for the door. Arkansas followed hurriedly. "Where you going?"

"See Ashford, find out what he wants me to do — bring in Dave or let it ride."

Brazil stepped out into the open, slowed as three men — Jake, the bartender at Joe Adams' saloon, and two others he had seen at the scene of the killing — moved toward him from the center of the street.

"We didn't see that killer with you when you rode in, Marshal," Jake said accusingly. "Told us you was going after him."

"I did," Luke replied laconically.

"But you somehow or other let him get away. Hell, I knew that's how it would be!"

From the doorway of the jail Arkansas snorted, said, "Now, why don't you keep that trap of your'n shut, Jake, unless you know what you're talking about?"

"Who says I don't? Brazil told us he was bringing in Ben Lockwood's kid for killing Joe — same as promised us he would if we'd simmer down. Well, we did, but he ain't done what he claimed he would. We're wanting to know why."

"We got us a pretty good idea why," one of the men with Jake said, nodding slowly.

"Never you mind about your —" Arkansas snapped, but checked his words as Luke stayed him with a raised hand.

"Don't lose any sleep over Dave Lockwood," the lawman said coldly. "He'll be here to stand trial for killing Adams."

"Maybe," Jake said, "and I don't figure folks here are going to cotton to waiting —"

"They'd better," Brazil said flatly in a promising sort of way and strode off toward Ashford's General Store.

Moriah's mayor, apparently seeing Luke

approaching, came out into the street and hurried forward. There was relief in his eyes as he wagged his head.

"Sure glad to see you! Was afraid you wouldn't make it back in time. There some trouble at Lockwoods?"

"Dave got away from me, rode off into the hills. I came back to get Arkansas. Aim to track him —"

Ashford frowned thoughtfully. "Best you let that ride. Right now, this voting is more important." He paused, drew forth a thick gold watch, consulted the Roman numerals on its face. "Six-thirty. We start in thirty minutes. I'd like for you and Arkansas to be there in case anybody tries voting that's not entitled. The two of you be enough?"

"Enough," Brazil said. "What about Dave Lockwood? He's a murderer —"

"Dave won't be going anywhere. Bringing him in can wait. Soon as the voting's over I'll have a talk with Ben, anyway. I think I can persuade him to have Dave turn himself in."

"Doubt if there's much chance of that," Luke said, glancing down the street. People were beginning to come in from the outlying areas, some in wagons, some in buggies, a few on horseback. "Where you going to hold the voting?"

"At the schoolhouse. We've let the children off for the day."

Brazil nodded. "I'll get myself a cup of coffee and get over there," he said, and beckoning to Arkansas, moved off for the Star Restaurant.

There was no trouble, probably due to the presence of Luke Brazil and Arkansas, who stood like sentinels at the doorway of the room in which the balloting was done and oversaw all who came to register their wishes.

The Lockwood family, except for Dave, of course, came as a party. With them were the Drapers, the Normans, and another rancher by the name of Kilgore. All voted — Ben Lockwood made the fact known in a loud voice — to close down the town to trail drives.

Jenny, passing by Luke on her way into the room, kept her eyes straight ahead, but Ben, a half smile on his lips as if remembering Luke's experience in the yard when he sought to follow Dave, nodded and said, "Howdy, Marshal."

And those of the settlement who believed as the rancher did, had their way. The door to the polls was shut promptly at noon and the counting began. Less than an hour later, John Ashford, with the town clerk, appeared to make the announcement.

"The vote is in favor of closing," he said, and after the burst of cheers that followed, added aside to Brazil, "I think it's a mistake, but that's how the majority wants it."

From nearby, Arkansas, gaze on the crowd milling about in the schoolyard, asked, "How you figure Cody Hungerford's going to take this?"

"Afraid there'll be plenty of trouble, far as he's concerned," Ashford said. "I think we can bank on it. Marshal, I expect you'd best get those signs made and put up as soon as you can. That hostler of McKenzie's will do it for you. Tell him the town will pay for them. I'd put up four — one at each side of the town, a mile or so out. Want to give the trail bosses time to swing off."

"If they will," Arkansas murmured.

Ashford shrugged. "Same as being a law now; they'll have to or face arrest," he said and turned toward his store.

Arkansas watched the man move off, hawked, spat into the loose dust. "Sure is mighty easy for him to say something like that, but it'll be you and me that'll be doing the facing up for the town — that is, if you aim to keep on wearing that star."

"Said I'd keep it on till they found somebody else. Gave my word."

"Yeh, so I recollect — but I'm wondering just how dang hard they're looking!"

"Hasn't been much time for it," Luke said, and put his glance on a surrey wheeling out of town.

Jenny and her mother were on the rear seat. Ben Lockwood, appearing well pleased and taking up most of the front, held the lines. Brazil had hoped for a chance to speak with the girl, but both times at the schoolhouse she had stonily passed him by, making it clear she had no such wish. He watched the vehicle until it made the bend at the end of the street, and then beckoned to Arkansas.

"Let's get that hostler busy on those signs," he said, starting toward the livery stable. "Sooner they're up, the less trouble we're likely to have."

Arkansas fell in beside the lawman, matched his long stride. "What about Dave Lockwood? Ain't we going after him?"

"You heard what Ashford said. Figures he can talk Ben into letting Dave come in on his own."

"You believe that?"

"Hardly, but it's the mayor who's calling the shots and I reckon he's entitled to try. Him and Lockwood are pretty good friends."

"Well," Arkansas said heavily, "I'm only hoping they get something worked out before Jake and some of them yahoos that're always hanging around Adams' place take it in their heads to go after the boy themselves."

"That's bothering me, too," Brazil said

as they turned into McKenzie's, "but not much we can do about it yet. Have to take it one step at a time, and if Jake and the others start something, it'll be up to us to stop it."

Luke paused. Two men, in the center of a quickly gathering crowd, were trading blows in front of Jergens' General Store, almost directly opposite. Pivoting, suddenly completely out of patience, the lawman roughly shouldered his way through the onlookers and broke the two men apart. Both were bleeding — one from a smashed nose, the other from crushed lips.

"Voting's over," Brazil said harshly. "There'll be no more fighting on the street —"

"May be over, but it sure'n hell ain't done with!" the man with the bloody nose declared. "It wouldn't've gone the way it did if them Box B cowhands hadn't put the fear of God in a lot of the folks."

"That's a goddam lie, Marshal! He's sore because him and —"

Brazil waved the man to silence, put his attention on the other combatant. "You want to come over to my office and sign a complaint against the ones you claim did that?''

Luke recognized the man as a homesteader from along the lower end of Dead Ute Creek, but he was not aware of his name.

"Nope, I ain't about to," the man said flatly, dabbing at his nose with a bandanna. "I aim to keep on living around here — and besides, I got kids to raise."

"Then, you best keep talk like that to yourself unless you're willing to back it up," Brazil said. "The voting was done fair and square. I was there all the time."

"Not talking about out at the schoolhouse, talking about here in town this morning. And it wasn't only them Box B cowhands, was some from the other ranches too —"

"Offer's still open," Luke said. "I'm willing to do something about it if you'll sign a complaint and give me some names."

The homesteader stuffed his bandanna back into a pocket, turned away. "Nope, let somebody else do it. Was plenty others here that got told what to do."

The question of why it was so important to Ben Lockwood that the town close its railhead to the trail drivers once again presented itself to Luke Brazil — and as before he found himself at a loss to come up with a reasonable answer. It was as if —

"Luke — look who's riding in," Arkansas said in a low voice.

Brazil came about, threw his glance to the end of the street, swore softly. Two riders: Cody Hungerford and a well-known gunman named Jack King.

13

Luke Brazil walked slowly out into the street, which was suddenly becoming deserted. Hungerford, a large, red-haired, bushy-bearded man who seemed to overflow the big, double-rigged Texas saddle he sat, drew up slightly and began to veer his horse toward the lawman.

King, the physical opposite of the rancher, was a small, lean, sly-faced man with flat, colorless eyes that flicked from side to side without any visible movement of his head. He was an arm's length behind Hungerford, apparently not wishing to block the cattleman's arrogant, pressing consideration of the town.

As the riders drew to a halt facing Luke, the silence that gripped the settlement seemed to grow more intense, and tension became as tangible as the driving, afternoon heat.

"Appears you're the law here." Cody Hungerford's voice boomed along the store fronts, reached everyone along the dusty roadway.

"I am."

The rancher shifted on his saddle, brushed at the sweat on his face. Leaning forward, he squinted at Luke through small, sun-rimmed eyes.

"I know you?"

"Name's Brazil."

The rancher settled back. "Ain't what I asked. I know what you're called. We ever met?"

"Not that I recollect," Luke replied.

"Expect you know me —"

"You're Cody Hungerford."

"Good, saves me a lot of jawing," the cattleman said and jerked a thumb at the gunslinger waiting quietly close by. "This here's Jack King. Reckon you've heard of him, too."

Brazil nodded indifferently, brushing the gunman aside as if he were unworthy of notice.

King spat over his shoulder, glared at

the lawman. "Badge toter, if you don't know who I —"

"I know who you are," Brazil said, and as the gunman's jaw tightened, shifted his attention to the rancher.

"I've been expecting you, Hungerford . . . but not for a few days yet."

"Wasn't planning to get here this soon myself," Cody Hungerford replied, glancing about, "but I run into an old friend that'd just been here."

"Sobel?"

"Yeh. Told me something about this here town not wanting drovers to —"

"True," Brazil cut in. "People voted this morning. This railhead's closed to all trail herds."

Hungerford received the information in silence. Off in the distance, crows were cawing noisily, and over across the dead line, in Perdition, two quick gunshots flatted hollowly in the hush.

"Is that a fact?" he said with a half smile, and looked at King. "What do you think of that, Jack? Ain't it a real shame!"

The gunman stirred on his saddle, let

his hands drop to the bone-handled pistols — one on each hip — that he was wearing.

"It sure is, Cody —"

"There'll be signs posted out on the trail before the day's over," Brazil said. "You'll have to swing your herd east, push it on to Trinity Crossing."

"Nope, guess not," Hungerford said easily.

Brazil shrugged, but his eyes narrowed slightly. He had expected trouble from Hungerford; here now was the flat declaration laid down in three brief words of deadly portent. "It's the law. I'll see to enforcing it."

Jack King laughed. "He sure don't know us, does he, Cody!"

The cattleman was studying Luke in a thoughtful, unrelenting way. After a moment he reached up, pushed his peaked high-crowned hat to the back of his head, again wiped at the sweat gathered on his brow. The silence that held the town deepened as, all along the street, those behind doors and windows listened and watched.

"Got a feeling Ben Lockwood had something to do with this damn-fool law," Hungerford said, at length.

"He had a vote —"

"Expect there was more than that. He's been looking to throw a kink in my rope for years. Reckon he thinks he's done it."

Luke shook his head. "I don't know what you're talking about," he said coldly, "and whatever's between you and Lockwood's your business. The town don't want trail hands running loose in it any more. Not only been too much damage, but the marshal got killed — and there's other folks who got hurt."

"Jesse Hurley getting his was an accident," Hungerford said angrily. "Probably was his own damned fault — but that ain't neither here nor there. I ain't letting Ben Lockwood put the chingus on me, not in my own town. Was me that started this place, and I sure'n hell ain't giving it up!"

"It's closed to you and your drovers — and any others that come along," Luke said quietly. "Better get that in your head, Hungerford."

Jack King, both palms on the horn of his saddle, leaned forward. "You figure you can keep us out?"

Features cold, expressionless, Luke Brazil said, "It'll be my job."

"Your last one, maybe," the gunman said softly.

"Maybe," Luke echoed.

Hungerford, florid face clouded, appeared to be unsure of what he'd been told. He clawed at his beard, again adjusted his tall hat.

"Just don't make no sense — folks letting Ben Lockwood rim-ram them into a loony deal like this! Hell, if the herds quit coming here this place'll dry up and blow away! Railroad ain't going to stand for it, either. They won't keep no spur track running in just for Lockwood's cattle and the little jags that the rest of them two-bit outfits around here want to ship."

"You're wasting your breath on me, Hungerford," Brazil said wearily. The long hours with only brief snatches of sleep — and that while he was in the saddle — were at last catching up with him, turning him irritable and short on patience. "The law will be enforced — you can count on it."

Cody Hungerford stared at Luke woodenly. "I see. Well, here's my side of it," he said in a low but strong voice. "I ain't swinging my herd east to Trinity Crossing. I'm bringing it here — using the pens I helped to build and loading the cars that're setting on the spur track I talked the railroad into building.

"And when the loading's done my crew'll get paid off, same as they always do, and then they'll be on their own to raise whatever hell they want. I'll try to keep them on the other side of the line, just like I always have, but if a few of them takes a notion to see what it's like over here, then I reckon they will. And you know what? Thinking about what this town's trying to do to me, I don't give a goddam —"

"Turn your herd east, Hungerford, take it to Trinity Crossing," Brazil said, his words cutting through those of the cattleman. "You won't find anything here now but trouble."

Cody Hungerford laughed derisively. "From you? From one lousy lawman? Hell, I've been eating your kind for supper twice a week ever since I growed up!"

"I'll say it once more," Brazil stated evenly, "this town's closed to you. Don't try forcing my hand."

"It's you that's forcing mine," Hungerford replied, nodding to Jack King, and as the pair swung their horses about and started off down the street, the rancher looked back over his shoulder and called softly, "I'll be back."

14

Cody Hungerford let his hard, pushing gaze settle on Jack King as they rode slowly along the street.

"I was looking for you to take care of that jasper," he said, accusation in his tone.

The gunman's stolid expression did not change. "Wasn't sure that's what you was wanting."

Hungerford laughed. "Like hell! What got into you, anyway? You see a bullet with your name on it in his eyes?"

King shrugged. Sweat beaded his forehead but he was ignoring it. "He's just another badge toter, that's all he is."

"Sure, sure — but I ain't faulting you none. Man sees he's stepped off into quicksand, he's smart to walk easy. And I ain't a bit bashful in saying it right out, there's something about that Brazil that makes you do a little double thinking. You for certain you ain't never run into him before? He's got all the earmarks of a hired gun."

"Stranger to me. If he was much shucks I'd know him."

"Yeh, reckon. But this is mighty big country and he could've blowed in from some other part — maybe Idaho, or Oregon."

"I'd know him if he was somebody fast with an iron," King said stubbornly.

Hungerford pulled off his hat, ran stubby fingers through his shock of red hair as he glanced along the street. There were several broken windows and considerable other damage, he saw; it appeared Parley Sobel's crew did have themselves a hell of a big time.

One of them had even got himself killed, he recalled Parley had said — and by that new marshal. The rancher frowned. That Brazil was a hard sonofabitch, he could see that, and while, ordinarily, he personally never backed away from trouble of any sort, just maybe this time he'd best give it some thought.

Nobody had ever accused him of being a fool.

But he wasn't about to let Moriah slam its gates on him. It meant adding a couple of weeks to the drive and knocking down the value of every steer a couple of dollars or more — all depending on how good the grass was between there and Trinity Crossing and how late he was getting his beef to market. On the other hand, he'd need to walk soft; he wasn't up against some stove-in lawman who was all wind and reputation and past the day when he was something to be reckoned with.

This Brazil had better not be taken lightly, not by anybody, but he would have to be dealt with. And that's where Jack King came in; handling such matters was his job, was why he was drawing a hundred a month and found.

Cody glanced about again. He could see faces behind the windows left untouched by Sobel's bunch — strained, fearful faces. He grinned knowingly. The town was scared, there was no doubt of that; like as not, it already repented letting that four-flushing Lockwood hooraw them into

185

voting to close the trail.

Hell, Moriah was his town — always had been, would continue to be so until he was planted six feet deep in the boneyard. That bunch there doing the voting were all Johnny-come-latelies as far as he was concerned. He'd all but built the railhead himself, and it had been he and his drovers that'd kept it alive those first few years. But just like some wet-nosed kid, it'd gone and got too big for its britches — and like a kid, it had a good licking coming so it'd straighten out and realize who the range bull was around there.

And that included Ben Lockwood, too. He needed jacking up plenty; and he sure as hell was going to get it, right along with the rest of the town, because the whole thing had to be his doings. He had a score of long standing to settle with Lockwood, had actually passed up the opportunity several times in the years since they'd left Texas, for the sake of Ben's family — but no more. This was it. This time he'd show Ben Lockwood up for what he was, once and for all.

Hungerford drew his horse to a stop.

They had reached the creek, the dead line separating the respectable part of town, as he'd heard it termed, from the hell raisers, the fancy women, and the card sharps.

"I'm heading on back to the herd," he said, facing King. "I'll be back in the morning with all the boys I can spare. Parley and his bunch'll be along, too."

"Aiming to teach this here dump a thing or two, that it?"

"You can put odds on it. I ain't about to let Ben Lockwood and them friends of his root me out of my own town! I want you to go on over, see Jed Tillman, ask him about that new marshal, Brazil —"

"Why?"

"Why! Dammit, the way you're pussyfooting around, you think I need answer that? But I've already said I don't blame you. If I was in your boots I'd be wanting to know more about him before I took him on too."

King was staring at the rancher with his flat, cold eyes. "You saying I —"

"Only saying what's smart. Jed'll be able to tell you all you want to know about him. Point is, I want Brazil out of the way. It don't make a damn to me how you do it; just get it done. Savvy?"

"Sure, Cody. Ain't you stopping by Jed's for a drink before you head back?"

"Nope, I'll do my drinking tomorrow, after I've got things squared up," Hungerford said and swung his horse around. *"Adios."*

"So long," King replied as the rancher rode off.

15

Hungerford had been reading his mind, Jack King realized as he roweled his horse and started him across the bridge for Perdition. Cody could see that he was being a mite careful when it came to Brazil — but there was something about the lawman that raised the danger signals within him and called for caution. Even Hungerford, hard-nosed as he was and accustomed to running roughshod over everybody and anybody, had pulled in his horns.

But that was neither here nor there. It was his job to take care of such problems for the rancher, and he would — doing it in his own way. Hell, he hadn't lived thirty years without using his head! He'd gone up against some of the best before he'd signed with Cody Hungerford, as

189

well as since, and he'd always come out on top — alive.

Now, he wasn't meaning to brag, but a man sure couldn't do that if he was a sucker — or a damn fool. He had to know exactly what he was doing, who he was standing up to, and what his chances were ahead of time, and handle the situation accordingly, which now and then called for a bit of trickery.

But so what? Stay alive. A man won by doing whatever was necessary. That was one thing he liked about working for Cody Hungerford; the rancher understood and never criticized the way he got a job done. He was interested only in the end result.

King looked up as a voice hailed him from the street. He nodded briefly, not bothering to see who it was, and moving on past the Alamo Saloon, swung in to the long rack that fronted the Horsehead. Dismounting, he secured the black he was riding and, stepping up onto the saloon's porch, crossed and entered.

The place, as usual, was crowded, and smoke hung in flat, blue-gray layers above the tables, the bar, and the dance floor, where several cowhands were wrestling back and forth with their heavily rouged and powdered women partners to the barely audible plink of a piano.

Evidently the patrons of the Horsehead weren't particularly disturbed by the town's decision to close and thus bring about the possibility of their favorite hangout's going out of business. But he reckoned it would make no difference over all, anyway; the gamblers, the doxies, and the hangers on would simply move to greener pastures, where they would find ample patronage awaiting them.

Pushing back his hat, King sleeved away the sweat on his forehead, and reaching out, grasped one of the girls passing close to him by the arm and pulled her roughly about.

"Where's Jed?"

The girl, small, worn-looking, wearing a low-cut, revealing purple dress, swore deeply and pulled away from him.

"You think I'm a horse or something, jerking me around like that?" she demanded, rubbing her arm.

"I know what you are," Jack replied coolly. "I asked you where Jed was."

The girl drew back slightly, recoiling from his manner. "Back room, I reckon. I don't keep track of him," she said, pointing at a door in the rear of the saloon.

The gunman pushed her aside, began to shoulder his way through the crowd, reaching the back wall shortly. Stepping up to the door, King grasped the knob and, disdaining to knock, pushed open the panel. It was Tillman's office, and the saloon man, sitting in a chair behind a table that served as a desk, head thrown back, was sleeping.

King, from a habit born of caution, closed the door behind him and crossed to Tillman. Grinning tightly, he slapped the top of the table sharply with his left hand and stepped back.

The saloon man came awake with a start. "What —"

King, smile broadening, faced him from the opposite side of the desk. "You do your sleeping in the daytime nowadays, Jed?"

Tillman squinted at the gunman, leaned forward, and then settled back wearily in his chair. "Howdy, Jack. Was a long night; trying to catch up on a few winks. What're you doing here?"

"Working for Cody Hungerford —"

"Cody!" Tillman echoed, frowning as he came to his feet. "He outside, at the bar?"

"Be riding in tomorrow morning with a bunch of his boys and some of Parley Sobel's outfit. He ain't taking kindly to the way the town's acting."

A satisfied look crossed Jed Tillman's face as he again relaxed in his chair. "Knew Cody'd be taking it personal. Tried to tell a lot of them folks over there he would and that they'd not get away with what they was doing, but they wouldn't listen. They were paying attention only to Ben Lockwood and some of them Holy Rollers . . . Cody want me to do something?"

"No, he'll be coming with all the help he'll be needing. It's me that's looking for information."

Tillman cocked his head to one side,

193

listened to the thump and hubbub beyond the door for a moment. "On what?"

"New marshal over there: Brazil. Me or Cody, neither one knows him."

"He ain't the regular badge. Old man that was, got hisself killed by one of Sobel's boys. Brazil — front name's Luke — is doing some ranching southeast of here. They sort of drafted him into taking the job till they could find somebody regular."

"Where'd he come from?" King asked idly, studying the scene on a whiskey company calendar hanging on the wall behind Tillman.

"Ain't sure. Like most of his kind, just sort of drifted in here from a little bit of everywhere. He's been a lawman — a bounty hunter, too, know that. A real tough sonofabitch, it's said, and anybody I ever heard of tangling with him come out on the short end."

"He fast with a gun?"

"Can't answer that straight, because I plain don't know, but I reckon he must be, else he wouldn't still be walking around after what he's been."

"Maybe. Cody wants him out of the way—"

"Where'd he bump into Brazil?"

"Up in town a bit ago. He served notice on us that the town was closed. It was about the first time I ever seen Cody Hungerford sort of ease off. Usually'd tell somebody like him to go to hell and then ride right over him."

Tillman nodded sagely. "Cody Hungerford ain't never been one to misjudge a man. You going after Brazil?"

"Expect so, I was sort of hoping you could wise me up a bit on him first, however."

Jed Tillman considered the gunman through half-closed, calculating eyes. "Reckon everybody looks for an edge," he murmured, "but I don't blame you. I'd sure hate to be the one calling out Luke Brazil."

"I reckon I can hold my own with him," Jack drawled, "but it's always been a rule of mine to find out all I could about a man, see if he's got a soft belly or something that'll make the job easier. He ain't no special friend of your'n, is he?"

"Hell, no!" the saloon man said, rocking forward. "I'll be the first in line to spit in his grave while they're planting him — if you get the job done."

"I will."

Again Tillman settled back, became thoughtful. After a minute of silence he nodded. "Yeh, I think maybe I got something that'll make it easy for you, Jack. Real easy."

King leaned back against the wall. Arms crossed, he waited for the saloon keeper to continue. When no words came from the man, he swore impatiently.

"Come on, Jed, I'm listening."

"Just this. Ben Lockwood's boy killed a man over there yesterday, then lit out for the hills. Brazil went after him, but he had to give up the hunt because of the voting and such. Probably aims to go after him in the morning."

"So —"

"Brazil's sweet on the boy's sister. I was thinking we could send word from her to Brazil saying the boy — his name's Dave — wants to give hisself up but's scared to come in on his own. There's been some lynch talk."

Jack King was nodding. "So the marshal goes out somewhere to meet the kid, only I'm waiting there for him instead. That what you got in mind?"

"That's what I'm thinking —"

"I don't figure this Brazil for a dummy. You think he'll swallow it?"

"Sure. Him and the gal's going to marry up. He'll be ascared not to believe it."

"You got some special place to send him to?"

"Yeh, the old Wicker cabin. It's a couple hours' ride from here on the road west."

"Sounds about right. How long'll it take you to fix things up? It's getting close to dark now."

"Plenty of time. You head on out. I'll have one of the girls take the message to Brazil — can tell her some cowhand brought it in to me. That way, she won't know no difference. Expect I'd best hold off a bit, though; give you a chance to get out there. That suit you?"

King shrugged. "Suits me fine," he said

and moved toward the exit. "About two hours west, you say?"

"That's it — an old log cabin. It'll be on your right, some off the road. Ain't been lived in for years, excepting for a drifter holing up overnight now and then."

"I'll find it," the gunman said and, opening the door, stepped back into the noisy confusion filling the saloon.

16

"You know her?" Brazil asked, watching the garishly dressed woman move through the doorway of his office, out into the dimly lit street.

"Sure," Arkansas replied. "Name's Mary Blue. Works for Jed Tillman, over at the Horsehead. Figured you'd seen her around."

Luke moodily considered the section of the street visible to him through the window. He had managed a few minutes' sleep, and eaten his evening meal, and was feeling somewhat rested.

The town was unusually quiet for that hour, and he guessed most folks were sticking close to home in fear of Cody Hungerford and his trail hands; but he reckoned they didn't need to worry about that yet — not before morning, anyway.

Best thing they could do was forget about them for the time being and prepare themselves for the day to come. That was what he had intended to do, but now this visit from Mary Blue was going to make him change his plans.

"Don't go around the Horsehead much," he said. "Tillman and me ain't exactly close friends."

Arkansas said, "Sort of slipped my mind. You believe what that gal said?"

"Giving it thought —"

"Well, you're plain loony if you do. Smells clean to hell like a put-up job to me! If Dave Lockwood wanted to give hisself up, why don't he just ride in? It'll be plenty dark in another half hour or so."

"Could be scared to risk it. Is a chance he could run into somebody that'd set up a holler."

"Yeh, suppose he could — but why didn't his sister just ride in, tell you? Why'd the lady have to give the message to some cowhand that happened to be riding by? I'm betting it's some kind of a trick — a ambush, maybe."

"Possible," Brazil said, almost indifferently. "But I can understand why Jenny wouldn't want to talk to me. We came to a parting of the ways —"

"Yeh, and I'm saying again I'm sorry — but there's something else that's a frazzing me: Why'd that cowhand take the message over to the Horsehead? Why didn't he drop it by here? Weren't none out of his way."

"You're forgetting how it is with a lot of men that're on the move. They aim to stay as far away from a lawman as possible — want nothing to do with them. Can remember a few times when you and me felt the same."

Arkansas drew out his bandanna, mopped wearily at his seamy face. "Can see I been doing all this jawing for nothing. You're believing it."

"It could be the truth just as easy as it could be some kind of a trap. Point is, Arky — I can't afford to ignore it."

"And you're going to ride out there —"

"Only take a couple hours or so, each way — and if it turns out there's nothing to it I'll rest easy. Seems I ought to be

201

doing something about Dave, anyway. Ashford got nowhere with Lockwood. Ben claimed he didn't know where the boy'd gone — and tomorrow's liable to be busy —"

Arkansas had dug into a pocket, produced a plug of tobacco, and was gnawing off a corner. Storing the wedge in the side of his mouth, he shook his head.

"You're saying riding out there to Wicker's'll make you rest easy; hell, Luke, you could wind up resting permanent! It won't be no chore a tall for some jasper to be waiting off in the dark — there's a lot of trees and brush around that cabin — until you show up and then putting a couple of bullets in you."

"Who? Hungerford's about the only man around that'd maybe have that in mind — and he won't be back until tomorrow. That herd of his is at least a day south, according to that stagecoach driver."

"He ain't going to be waiting for the herd. He'll leave it grazing somewheres, get hisself together a gang of them drovers, and come on in. But, like you're saying, that'll probably be tomorrow. I'm thinking about them two galoots that you threw in the calaboose — that pair that was riding for Sobel.''

Brazil stirred. ''Rufe and Slim, friends of Garret. Hadn't given them any thought.''

''Well, you better! You planted their partner, and they've already tried once to square up with you for doing it. There ain't no guarantee they won't be trying it again.''

The lawman rubbed at his jaw. ''It don't fit, Arky. I doubt if either one of them knows about the old Wicker place. It's too far out of town for them to've just run across it. And they're Texans. They came up from the south, not the west.''

''Now you're tromping on your own self! Just got through telling me there's a chance this here message that drifter brought in is on the level. Same goes for them two drovers. There's a chance they're behind this and are laying out there at the old cabin waiting to shoot you full of holes. Could be wrong — but like you're saying — there's a chance I ain't."

Brazil considered that in silence. Somewhere along the street a horse, neglected too long by its rider, whickered anxiously.

"I'll keep a sharp eye out," the lawman said, coming to his feet. "You going to do your sleeping here in the jail?"

"I ain't sleeping nowhere — I'm riding out there with you," the older man said resignedly, coming to his feet. "Two of us watching out'll be better'n one."

Brazil, pulling on his hat, paused, studied Arkansas with a half smile. "You're like an old mama quail looking out for a lone chick lately. I'm obliged, but there's no need for you to come."

"Maybe not, but if it's all the same to you, I will anyways. . . . Owe you from way back, Luke — for that time in Laredo. I ain't never forgetting that —"

"I don't keep books," Luke cut in. "You don't owe me anything."

"It's me that's doing the bookkeeping," Arkansas said, and added, "You want me to trot down to McKenzie's and get the horses?"

"I'll meet you there. Like to make the rounds before I leave, be sure everything's locked up."

Arkansas grinned, reached for the lamp, and turned down the flame to a lower level. "Ain't no doubt of that! Folks here are like a bunch of prairie dogs with a couple of coyotes hanging around. They ain't poking their heads out for nobody. . . . See you at the livery stable."

A half hour later, they were in the saddle and moving at a steady pace over the well-traveled road that bore directly westward. There was no talk between them, both having said all that was necessary back in the marshal's office and during the few minutes at McKenzie's stable. Now it was simply a matter of getting to the old, abandoned cabin and determining if there was any truth to the message the drifting cowhand had brought in — one supposedly from Jenny Lockwood.

It was a fine, warm night. Despite scatterings of fleecy clouds, a strong moon flooded the flats and slopes with lights and left only the areas where pines and firs grew thick deep in shadows. A night bird of some sort sang off in the distance, and well to the north, in the low piñon-and-cedar studded short hills that bubbled smoothly on to eventually merge with the towering Skulls, coyotes had set up a chain chorus of discordant yapping.

He'd be glad when this was all over, Brazil thought as they loped on through the night. He wanted to get back to his ranch, to the business of raising cattle — and, he hoped, straightening out the misunderstanding with Jenny.

If she had been the one to send word concerning her brother Dave, it was a good sign. At least she was talking to him — after a fashion — and possibly had come to understand his position better. Of course, if it was all a hoax, an ambush, as Arky suspected, then matters between them were likely right where they had been: at a stalemate.

Surely it was possible to talk it out. The vote to close the town had been what Ben Lockwood wanted, and it had gone his way. The fact that he had opposed the idea shouldn't be permitted to stand between them. They'd had other differences since meeting, and undoubtedly there would be times in the future — assuming one lay ahead for them — when they'd disagree. It was only normal, natural, a part of living. He'd try to make Jenny see that — if she would give him the opportunity.

But it could be difficult. Ben Lockwood was not one to forget and forgive. He'd always remember that he had been opposed, openly, and the fact that his daughter had been on the verge of marrying a man who had bucked him no doubt was a source of embarrassment.

Too, there was the problem of Dave. Since he was Jenny's brother, guilty or not, he posed a problem for him. He was duty bound to bring the boy in and lock him up to await trial for murder, no matter what the situation. How would Jenny look upon that?

Would she stand by Dave regardless, and in so doing resent him, as a lawman, for bringing her brother up before a judge to answer the charge? She shouldn't blame him, of course, but, as a rule, blood ties overrode reason, and he was prepared to go unsurprised if that was the way it turned out.

But he intended to talk to Jenny, try to make her forget how her father, burdened with insulted pride, felt toward him, and understand his obligation to the job he had assumed, if she would allow it. Jenny had to realize that it was only a matter of sheer luck that it fell to his lot to go after and bring in Dave for the killing of Joe Adams.

It could easily have been Marshal Jesse Hurley, had he not sustained the misfortune of stopping a stray bullet, or any of a half dozen other men who, after the death of the old lawman, happened to be available. But as it was —

"We're here."

Arkansas's words came to Luke above the quiet thud of the horses' hoofs in the deep dust of the road. Glancing up, he saw the squat silhouette of the sagging old structure, barely visible among the tall pines and lesser growth a short distance to their right.

"Don't see no light," Arkansas muttered in a dissatisfied voice as they halted at the edge of what had once been a clearing. Now overgrown with gooseberry, rabbitbush, mahogany, and such, it was little more than a band of shrubbery, but of lesser height.

"Not likely to be showing one," Brazil said, striving to make out dark outlines in the blackness beyond the low building. "Can see a horse off there in the back, maybe two. Could be Jenny and Dave's."

"And they could belong to them two drovers —"

"Maybe nothing at all, too," Brazil said. "Could be just shadows. Let's go on in."

"Easy like, now!" Arkansas said hurriedly in a low whisper. "Let's don't go wading in there like a couple of greenhorns at a fandango. You head around to the back, see if them are Lockwood horses, while I snake around to the front, have a look. Maybe that way we can find out what we're up against."

Brazil nodded, started moving. "Watch yourself," he warned softly.

17

Working in close, Brazil halted a few yards from the cabin and dismounted. He could see the area at the rear of the weathered old structure more clearly now, and could definitely make out one horse. There might be a second farther over, but he could not be sure. If there wasn't, it meant nothing; Jenny could have returned to the ranch.

Quiet, keeping in the brush, Luke circled slowly in to where he was only a stride from the animal stirring nervously at his stealthy approach. The horse was dark — a bay, or perhaps even a black. The brand —

The sudden crack of pistol shots coming from in front of the cabin brought Brazil up short. Arkansas! He had run into trouble! Cursing, the lawman drew his pistol, started along the side of the cabin at a hard run. The old man had been right: it was an ambush.

Drawing near the front of the cabin, Brazil slowed, ears straining to catch any sound, eyes struggling to pierce the darkness and reveal the source of the gunshots.

There hadn't been an exchange between Arkansas and the bushwhacker, he was certain of that. The reports appeared to be alike, as if coming from the same weapon, and the heavy, 44-caliber converted pistol Arkansas carried made a noise all its own when it was discharged. Brazil swore again as he proceeded cautiously along the wall. He shouldn't have let the older man go on by himself; they should have stayed together.

The corner of the cabin was no more than a step away. Luke paused, still listening intently. Somewhere on ahead in the dry weeds and brush there came a scraping noise. It could be Arky unhurt, or wounded, crawling off into the safety of the shadows. He'd best —

A surge of alarm rocked through Luke

Brazil. He started to pivot, face the slightest of sounds coming from behind him. In that next fragment of time he was aware of the flash of gunpowder, of a solid, shocking blow to the side of his head — and then all dissolved instantly into total blackness as he went down.

It was the cold that brought Brazil back to consciousness. He opened his eyes, felt the prick of stiff weeds against his skin, and raised his head with a jerk. Pain roared through him. Cursing, he hung motionless, allowed the pain to subside. Then, more slowly and with care, he began to lift himself again, his fog-shrouded brain fighting to bring understanding and awareness to him.

He was on his hands and knees. The cold was like a thick, deadening blanket, and he realized he was shivering. The thought, *it's early morning,* filtered through his mind. But it couldn't be! It was still dark and there were stars shining. The moon was gone, however, hidden by heavy clouds piling up in the west.

Head hanging, brain yet thick and only half functioning, Luke Brazil rode out the dragging minutes. Gradually full consciousness began to return. He settled back, sat flat on the ground, shoulders against the wall of the cabin, his slow, painful movements startling a field mouse or other small varmint in the weeds nearby and sending it scurrying off into the night.

The side of his head felt damp, sticky. Luke raised a hand, explored the area with his fingertips. Blood, he knew without having to see. Blood had a thick, gummy feel. He'd been shot, but the bullet had struck him a glancing blow along the temple.

That was it. Somebody — the bushwhacker — had gotten in behind him, had fired his weapon at almost point-blank range. But, thanks to the darkness and the fact that his intended target had whirled at the exact instant he'd pressed off the trigger of his gun, the killer had missed dead center and his bullet had delivered only a grazing wound.

Arkansas. . . . Brazil, pressing his weight against the side of the cabin for support, struggled to an upright stance. Arky was down somewhere in front of the cabin; otherwise he would have been heard from by then. How long had it been since the gunshots were fired? How long had he lain in the weeds? An hour at least, Luke reasoned; perhaps longer.

His senses were now clearing rapidly. Brazil reached up, pulled the bandanna from about his neck, and tied it around his thudding head. The wound over his temple had begun to bleed again; the pressure of the cloth, drawn tight, should halt the flow — at least until he could take time to better care for it.

His pistol . . . It was on the ground, in the weeds and dry grass where it had fallen when the bushwhacker's bullet had felled him. Squatting to avoid leaning over, which he knew would send him down flat on his face, Luke probed about in the sun-seared growth for the weapon. After a few moments, his fingers came upon the cool metal of the barrel, and grasping the pistol firmly, he again stood upright.

The bushwhacker could still be around. He'd best make certain one way or the other before he ventured out into the open in search of Arkansas. Turning about, Luke carefully, silently began to make his way along the wall of the cabin for the rear. If the horse he'd seen was gone, then he could be reasonably sure the man was also gone. Were there two horses? Thinking back, he doubted it; the other would have been close by, and he had seen nothing. Such would indicate there had been only one man waiting there to kill him. Who?

Brazil reached the back of the cabin, paused. The horse was not there. He nodded in satisfaction and, hurrying as best he could on legs that were still shaky, returned to the front of the structure and out into the yard.

He saw Arkansas immediately. The man was lying directly opposite the door of the cabin, about midway of the once-distinct hardpack. The bushwhacker had evidently opened up on Arky as he moved forward through the shadow cast by the structure.

Brazil, ignoring further caution and pain, rushed to the crumpled shape, knelt beside it. Arkansas was on his back, bowled over apparently by the impact of several bullets. The dark, sodden stain on his chest showed where the slugs had thundered into his body.

Slipping an arm under his friend, Luke raised him a few inches and felt for a pulse. It was there — slow and weak.

"Arky!" he said, putting his mouth close to the older man's ear.

The slack form stirred. "Yeh? That you, Luke?"

The reply had been almost inaudible. "It's me."

"He . . . he got me . . . good . . . I . . . I reckon. . . ."

"Who was it, Arky? Who got you?"

"Ain't sure. Was one fellow . . . never got no look at him but . . . but he looked like . . . like that gunnie that rode in . . . with Hungerford."

"King. Jack King."

"Yeh. Seen him . . . come out of the cabin . . . after he . . . potshot me . . . from inside. Run . . . for the horse . . . figured you'd jump . . . him."

Brazil was pressing back the anger that was roaring through him. Jack King — that was who it had to be. Hungerford was making ready for the coming day.

"I was alongside the cabin," he said, returning his attention to Arkansas. "Heard the shooting, was trying to get where I could see what was going on, when King slipped in back of me and took a shot. Only grazed me, but it knocked me cold for a spell . . . You lay quiet. I'll get the horses and we —"

"Be a waste of . . . time. We . . . both know I'm . . . a goner. Man's card . . . turns up . . . ain't nothing he can . . . do."

Brazil swore savagely under his breath. Why couldn't it have been him that went up against King, instead of his old friend? He should not have allowed Arkansas to go around in front alone; they should have stayed together —

"Luke. . . ."

Brazil's manner softened instantly at the faint voice. "Right here, Arky."

"You . . . you recollect that . . . time . . . down in . . . in San Antone?"

"San Antone?" Brazil repeated, raising the man's head a bit higher in an effort to make him more comfortable.

"Yeh . . . San Antone." Arkansas's voice was now very low, weak. "That there . . . circus thing . . . we went to. And them . . . them two hooly-hooly . . . girl dancers. . . ."

"I remember —"

"Can't seem . . . to think . . . of their names. Been trying. . . ."

The lawman again swore silently. There was nothing he could do for his old friend, and that realization served only to fan the anger whipping through him to a higher pitch. All he could do was wait, watch, as life ebbed slowly. The only good thing about it was that Arkansas was beyond the point of pain.

"Can't remember them either."

"No need. Was . . . only wondering. Was . . . you on that trail . . . drive to . . . to . . . Dodge in sixty-four . . . or maybe . . . it was Abilene. I ain't . . . sure . . . somehow."

Arky's mind was wandering, his thoughts rambling. Brazil smiled down at him. "Expect I was. We've been a lot of places together, old friend — rode a lot of miles."

218

"For certain. Sure do . . . hate . . . falling down . . . on you like I . . . I done. Ought've had . . . more sense'n to . . . to go sashaying . . . up to . . . that door."

"He was waiting for you — thinking you were me," Luke said. "You pretty sure it was Jack King?"

"Pretty sure . . . that hat . . . he was wearing. Recollect it. Know . . . what I . . . been thinking . . . laying . . . here, Luke? There's somebody . . . else got . . . a hand in this. King . . . he'd not know . . . about this place. And . . . and . . . he'd not . . . know about . . . the lady unless . . . ."

Arkansas's words trailed off. Brazil looked more closely at the man. In the pale light the skin of his face had taken on a dry, parchment look and his glazing eyes had retreated into deep pockets.

"Arky —"

The slight body stirred in Brazil's arms. "I . . . I sure . . . could use . . . a drink . . . partner." The words came falteringly, as if being dragged. "Even . . . even some of . . . that Mex rotgut

. . . we got that . . . time in . . . that doby saloon . . . in Santa Fe.''

The voice broke. Arkansas's body went limp, as his chin sank deeper into his chest. For a long minute Luke Brazil studied the slack features of his old friend, and then, laying him gently aside, he got to his feet, cold, driving anger pushing through him. He'd get the horses, take Arky back to town and then hunt up Jack King and settle with him.

The horses were in the trees off the upper corner of the yard. Arky's would be a bit to the right of his, he reckoned as he strode purposefully through the rank, weedy growth. Reaching the spot where he had left his mount, Brazil drew up short, puzzled. The bay was gone. He wheeled, crossed to where Arkansas's buckskin should be waiting. It, too, was missing.

At once Luke began to scout the area. Both animals could have strayed off while grazing. He doubted the gunshots had frightened either of them — both being far from strangers when it came to shooting.

An hour later Brazil gave up the search

and returned to the yard and Arkansas. The horses were gone, either deliberately driven off by King or, confused, had followed the gunman's mount when it had been ridden off. The latter was most likely, he figured — and the possibility of encountering either one or both of them on the way back to town was slim. They'd not stop until they reached the settlement, and he'd as well make up his mind he was in for a long walk.

Grim, head throbbing from the wound along his temple, Brazil picked up the body of Arkansas and carried it up to the cabin. The door was closed, and booting it open angrily, he entered and laid his friend on the pile of leaves and pine needles some tarrying drifter had carried in to make a pallet.

Wheeling, Luke returned to the entrance of the old structure. Pausing there, he looked back at the lifeless figure on the floor, barely visible in the darkness. Then, nodding slightly as if in final farewell, he closed the door and wedged the latch with a bit of wood to prevent its blowing open, and turned away.

As soon as he reached town — a hell of a long walk, he realized — he'd send Ed Feeney back for Arky. And then he'd go looking for Jack King.

18

Brazil could hear gunshots long before he reached the outskirts of Moriah, shortly after dawn. Bitter, angry, tired from the long walk from Wicker's cabin, he drew up finally at the rear of Jergens' General Store, and breathing hard for wind, made his way forward along the side of the store building to where he could have a look at the street.

Riders — undoubtedly drovers from the herd Cody Hungerford was bringing in and some he recalled as Parley Sobel's men — were racing back and forth firing their pistols at will. Dust and gunsmoke hung in the air, which was filled with the sounds of shattering glass, barking dogs, the rapid thud of hoofs, and the yells of trail drivers enjoying themselves.

Brazil could see none of the local

223

citizenry, guessed all had taken cover inside their stores and homes, nor could he find Jack King or Cody Hungerford among the riders harassing the town. But that was to be expected; the rancher and his hired gun would be flaunting their presence in one of the saloons, probably the Palace, having their drinks while the trail hands brought the town, as Hungerford would express it, to its senses.

He had to put a stop to it, and to do that he needed first to reach the jail — and the gunrack. A shotgun was the best weapon at times such as this. That meant crossing the street. Luke gave that a moment's sober thought, and then, reaching up, he unpinned his star and thrust it into a pocket. Drawing his pistol, he stepped out into the open.

Staggering, mimicking a drunk, firing his weapon into the air, he started across the street, shouting back at the riders who veered past him, cursing good-naturedly those who came too close. Employing such a ruse rankled him, but it was necessary he put the town's welfare first, and that salved his wounded pride, although it did increase the sullen anger boiling within him.

He reached the sidewalk without interruption, hurried to the jail. The door was closed — locked. Brazil swore. He'd left it open when he and Arkansas had ridden out to the Wicker place. Moving to the window, he cupped his hands over his eyes and peered through the dust-filmed glass. John Ashford was sitting at his desk, a dazed look on his face.

Brazil rapped sharply on the pane. Ashford started, sat up straight. The lawman knocked once more, pressed his face close to the window. At once, Moriah's mayor came to his feet and, hurriedly unlocking the door, admitted Luke.

"Marshal!" Ashford said with obvious relief. "I'm sure glad to see you alive! I thought they'd somehow managed to kill you," he added, closing the thick panel and again locking it.

Brazil, wordless, had crossed to the gunrack, was releasing the chain. "Got myself suckered into going out to Wicker's cabin," he said, taking down one of the double-barreled weapons. "Was an ambush."

"Can see you got hurt," Ashford said, pointing at the bandanna around Luke's head.

"Only a graze — nothing more," Brazil said, and paused. "Arkansas's dead."

"Arkansas! That's too bad, Marshal. You know who did it?"

"Jack King — that gunfighter Hungerford keeps at his side." Brazil had loaded the shotgun, was stuffing additional shells into his pockets. "How's it happen you're here?"

"Saw Hungerford and his crew ride in. Wasn't sure you did, so I left my place and came here to warn you in case you were catching up on your sleep. They started in their hell raising about then and I couldn't get back, so I locked the door and holed up, wondering all the time what had happened to you."

"Had to walk all the way back from Wicker's," Brazil said and moved toward the door. "You'll have to be my jailer. Pick yourself a shotgun and be ready to open up and let me in when I start bringing —"

"You're — you're going to arrest that bunch?" Ashford said in an incredulous voice.

"Only two ways to put a stop to what's going on out there," Brazil said, shrugging. "Arrest them or shoot them off the saddle. They'll get their choice."

Unlocking the door, Luke stepped out onto the landing. Two drovers on foot and coming down the center of the street offered the opportunity for the example he wished to set. Cradling the shotgun, he moved out to intercept them. Both slowed, eyed him narrowly, and stopped.

"You're under arrest," Brazil called, and fired a load of buckshot into the dust in front of them by way of emphasis.

The drovers yelled, jumped back. "Now, hold on, Marshal, we ain't —" one protested.

"Head for the jail!" Luke ordered, waving the double-barrel at them carelessly. "Next charge'll be coming at you belly high!"

Beyond them, Brazil could see that other drovers, having heard the blast of

227

the shotgun, were pausing, looking in his direction. And then, as the two men started hurriedly toward the jail, he glanced to the opposite end of the town. The shot could have drawn the attention of other Hungerford or Sobel men in that area, too.

"Inside!" he ordered, shoving the pair roughly as Ashford pulled back the door.

The drovers stumbled into the office, and John Ashford, weapon in hand, shepherded them into the first of the already open and waiting cells in the rear of the building. Closing and locking the grill, he returned hurriedly.

Brazil, standing in the doorway, was looking toward the Palace Saloon. The word of what he'd done would be reported swiftly to Cody Hungerford — and King. Both should put in an appearance shortly, and he would be spared the trouble of seeking the gunman out to square up for Arkansas.

Cool, calculating, as was his way in times past, Luke Brazil forethought the coming moments. First he'd take care of King — he was the dangerous one of the pair. When the gunfighter was down and no longer a threat he'd see to Cody Hungerford. A taut grin pulled at his lips. It seemed natural to be standing there waiting, figuring, planning, and the bright tension racing through his body was an old, familiar sensation — and not unwelcome.

The hard, quick pound of oncoming horses brought Luke's attention around. Four drovers, coming from across the dead line, were racing up. They came to a plunging stop in front of him. Unmoving, shotgun reloaded and hanging from the crook of an arm, Brazil faced them.

"Unbuckle your gun belts and let them drop," he said before any of them could speak.

The riders, momentarily taken aback, glanced at one another and then grinned broadly. One, a lean, hook-nosed man with yellow hair and mustache and wearing a fringed leather jacket, spat into the dust.

"Now, who the hell're you?"

Brazil remembered his star. Taking it from the pocket where he'd placed it, he pinned it on. "The town marshal," he replied quietly.

Again the drovers exchanged looks. The one in the leather jacket wagged his head. "He's the law, boys!" he said, laughing. "You hear what he's wanting us to do? Shuck our irons — that's what. I don't figure he knows what's going on around here."

"You tell him, Curly," one of the others said. "He must've been off hiding in a hole somewheres."

Curly spat again. "Mister Tin Star," he began with exaggerated politeness, "this here burg's been took over by Mister Cody Hungerford. He's the boss now, the old range bull, the big he-bear, and what he says goes. *Comprende?*"

"And he told us we was to have ourselves a time, doing whatever we took the notion to do," one of the others, a squat, scar-faced puncher said, "and I reckon that means them two friends of our'n you just throwed in your calaboose."

"We want them turned loose," Curly finished.

A humorless half smile pulled at Brazil's hard mouth. "You've got maybe thirty seconds left to shed those gun belts before I start shooting," he said.

Curly and his partners once again looked at each other, but their manner had undergone a drastic change. The cockiness had been replaced with concern, and as Brazil suddenly raised the level of the shotgun's twin barrels, the rider at Curly's left hastily reached for his buckle and released it.

"The dang fool means it!" he shouted in alarm as his gun and the belt fell to the ground.

The man called Curly shrugged in resignation, surrendered his weapon. Immediately, the two remaining riders got rid of theirs.

"You're going to have to do some answering to Mr. Hungerford for this," Curly said darkly. "He ain't going to like it one bit."

"I don't give a damn what he likes!" Brazil snapped. "Now climb down and march inside!"

Activity along the street had come to a

halt except for an altercation of some sort down near McKenzie's Livery Stable — a fight probably between two drovers or something, Luke supposed. He could see that several riders, their horses pulled to a stop, were watching him narrowly, apparently uncertain what they should do.

Ignoring them, Luke stepped aside as Curly and his three friends, mumbling threats, stomped past him and into the jail, where John Ashford escorted them on to a cell, and as the clang of the iron door reached him, shifted his glance back to the Palace Saloon.

There was still no sign of Hungerford or Jack King. There could be but one explanation of that: they were not there, were instead favoring one of the other saloons with their presence — and if not the Palace, the town's best, then it would be Tillman's, its counterpart across the line, in Perdition.

"By God, you're slowing them down aplenty!" Ashford said admiringly, coming out into the street and collecting the belts and weapons abandoned by the four drovers.

Brazil nodded. "Need to jug a few more," he said.

The horses that Curly and his friends had been riding were still at the rack, waiting uncertainly. The lawman moved up to them, and sweeping off his hat, sent them charging off in the direction of the dead line. Two drovers, coming out of Joe Adams' place at the moment the riderless mounts thundered by, drew up stiffly and focused their gaze on Brazil.

And then, together, they hurried to their own horses, swung into the saddle, and wheeling about with guns already drawn, pounded up the street for the lawman. A scant dozen yards away one triggered his weapon. Dust spurted over Brazil's boots.

Luke swung the double-barrel up smoothly, drove a load of buckshot over the heads of the approaching pair. The tall hat of the man to his left was caught by some of the pellets, was whipped off and sent spinning to the street. Both men yelled, pulled up short.

"Hey — what the goddam hell you think —"

"Drop your gun belts and come over

here," the lawman barked, "or I'll blow your damned heads off!"

The drovers complied quickly. Luke watched them enter the jail, heard the scuff of their boots and once again the clang of the cell door as Ashford closed and locked it behind them. Moving forward a few steps, Luke sent the two horses rushing off down the street, and picking up the weapons dropped by the pair, handed them to Ashford.

"Things are getting quieter by the minute," the mayor said. "But we're going to be running out of room if you haul in many more."

Brazil watched him toss the belted guns onto the pile building in a corner of the room, and settled on a corner of the desk. He was tired, and he could use a drink, but he knew he could think of neither at the moment. "They'll hold off now till Hungerford shows up, I expect," he said. "Need a little encouraging now from him."

Ashford had crossed the office, had taken a stand in the door. He stiffened, looked back at Brazil. "They won't have to wait long," he said in a strained voice. "Hungerford and a bunch of his drovers are coming in now — and they've got Ben Lockwood."

19

Brazil propped the shotgun he was holding against the wall of the jail, and stepping up beside John Ashford, eyed the approaching riders. The line of his jaw hardened as the old, familiar tension and heady excitement, reawakened so recently, surged full strength through him once more. Here was Jack — here was Hungerford — here now was the shootout — the test.

"What's happened? What are they doing to Ben?"

Ashford's words registered on Luke's mind. He put his attention on Lockwood. The rancher, hatless, disheveled, one sleeve of his shirt ripped, was riding between Cody Hungerford and King, while scattered around behind them were a dozen or so trail hands.

The lawman made no comment. He understood now why Hungerford and King had not come out on the street when he began arresting the drovers; they had gone to the Box B and made a prisoner of Lockwood. Apparently there had been a considerable fracas, judging from Lockwood's condition and the appearance of some of the drovers.

The party came slowly down the street, making a show for all to see. Hungerford and King each held a rein to the horse Lockwood was riding, and thus were keeping the man effectively pinned between them.

The ragged cavalcade drew abreast of the Antlers Hotel, more or less the center point of town, and came to a stop. Hungerford, now releasing his tie to Lockwood's horse, raised himself in his stirrups. A big man to begin with, he now loomed much larger.

"All you folks!" he called out in a loud voice. "I want you to listen!"

As the summons echoed along the street, several storekeepers appeared, some obediently, some reluctantly, along with a number of individuals who had been watching from the safety of the buildings. But the showing was thin, the majority of Moriah's residents preferring to take no chances and remain out of sight, if not of hearing.

"I want everybody to hear this!" Hungerford continued, and settled back on his saddle.

Brazil, arms folded across his chest, stepped out onto the landing and crossed to its forward edge. He saw Cody Hungerford straighten, frown, turn quickly to Jack King.

"I thought you told me he was out of it — dead."

The gunman was staring at Luke in disbelief. "Figured he was. Sure'n hell cut somebody down —"

"The wrong man," Hungerford said in disgust.

"No problem," King said, dropping the rein he was holding. "I can fix that right now."

Brazil, smiling thinly, took another step toward the party in the street. All had come to taut attention, were watching him closely. The excitement and tension within him mounted higher, and again the remembrance of times past, the pulsing moments of danger flowed through him, filled him with a strange sort of satisfaction.

And why not go back to that life? He had no future now, at least not the kind he'd planned for. Jenny no longer was a part of it, and the man he considered his best friend, Arkansas, was dead. He could turn the ranch over to the hired hands working it, let them pay him off as —

"Let it go — for now," Hungerford said, and then added to the men behind him, "Keep an eye on that marshal."

Luke remained taut, a rigid, unyielding figure facing the riders in the street, but he made no move to press Jack King. The odds were too great at the moment; he'd not only have the gunman to deal with now but the drovers Cody Hungerford had directed to watch him. But his time would come.

Elsewhere along the roadway more Hungerford trail hands were drifting up to take places with their friends. He spotted additional Sobel drovers among the men, guessed most of Parley's crew had waited over to take part in the hurrahing of the town.

"You folks — " Hungerford called in his booming voice, "I want to talk about you closing down the trail. Where's your mayor?"

There were a few moments of silence, and then John Ashford stepped through the doorway of the marshal's office and took a stand a few steps from Brazil on the sidewalk.

"Here —"

Hungerford leveled his gaze on the man. "Like to know your feelings on closing the town —"

"How I feel doesn't count," Ashford said, speaking up in a strong voice. "It's what the people living here wants that does — and they voted to close. That's how it will be — closed not only to you but every trail drive."

"You know why?" Hungerford asked. "You want to know the real reason why folks voted the way they did?"

Ashford nodded. "They're tired of the

way your trail hands acted —"

"That's not it at all!" the cattleman cut in. "It was Lockwood here that was behind it, pushing to get it done, and I went out and got him and brought him in so's he could tell you why."

Hungerford reached out, grasped Ben Lockwood by the arm and shook him roughly. "Speak right up. Tell them why you wanted it. Let them see the kind of a sneaking, lying bastard you are!"

A complete, stunned silence had settled over the street. More onlookers were now in evidence, Hungerford's words having brought them into the open. Ashford moved up alongside Luke Brazil, his features drawn to a puzzled frown.

"What's he talking about?"

The lawman shook his head. "Expect we'll know in a minute," he said, keeping his eyes on Jack King, whose burning attention upon him had not wavered. "Best you keep clear of me, Mayor. Like as not, things are going to bust loose here after a bit."

Ashford said, "I'm not hiding out. Took a little doing, but I've discovered I can stand up to any of them.''

"You're taking a chance out here — and you're not wearing a gun.''

"I can change that,'' John Ashford said, and retreated slowly toward the entrance to the jail.

"Seems old Ben here's a mite bashful,'' Hungerford was saying. "Just plain don't want to talk up, tell you folks why he wanted the town closed.

"Well, I'll tell you, then. So's he could hog it all, that's why. He wanted the railhead for himself and maybe a couple of his friends. Closing the town here means me and other trail bosses'll have to push our herds for another ten days or so, before we can get to where we can ship them. That's going to cost us not only all that extra time on the drive but it'll walk plenty more tallow off our steers, too.

"But Ben here won't have that problem. He'll be bringing his beef right to the pens here after maybe no more'n a fifteen- or twenty-mile drive. They've been fattening on good grass all spring and that short walk ain't going to lean them down one whit. They'll be in fine shape when they're loaded — what buyers call prime beef.

"And by the time I can get my steers to Trinity and loaded, Ben's'll already have reached the market, and being real prime and there a couple of weeks ahead of mine, they'll draw top prices.

"Now, that's why he was so all-fired set on seeing you vote to close the trail. He lied to you about his reason — same as he once lied to the woman I aimed to marry and run off with her himself. It was down in Texas, and she was the prettiest — But that ain't got nothing to do with now, other'n to prove he's a liar and don't give a goddam for nobody but himself. Speak up, Ben, tell the folks I'm speaking pure gospel!"

Brazil caught motion at the end of the street and frowned. A buggy had whirled into view. It was Jenny Lockwood and her mother. The horse, flecked with lather, had evidently come all the way from the Box B at a dead run.

Hungerford reached out again, slapped Lockwood, slumped in his saddle, soundly on the back. "Come on, Ben! This ain't no time to show your tail feathers. I've got you roped and tied. You might as well admit to the folks what a lying four-flusher you are.''

Luke watched Jenny drive the buggy into the vacant lot between the Antlers and Jergens' General Store, and come to a halt. The girl leaped from the seat, turned to assist her mother.

"We're all awaiting," Hungerford said in his jeering voice. "You say your piece, Ben: tell the folks what I said was true. Then we'll all go have us a drink. It's hot setting here in the sun, and my boys're getting sort of itchy, but they're figuring same as me that watching you eat dirt'll be worth it.''

"I'm going to stop this," Brazil said, hearing Ashford move in close to him again.

He glanced over his shoulder. Moriah's mayor not only had strapped on one of the gun belts and pistols taken off the drovers he'd locked in the cells, but was carrying a shotgun as well.

"Best hold off a bit," Ashford said. "Let Ben speak up. I want to know if what Hungerford says is the truth. I expect the rest of the town would, too."

"We're still waiting, Mister Lockwood!"

As Cody Hungerford's words echoed along the street, Brazil's attention swung to the hotel, to the porch extending across its front. Jenny and her mother had appeared, looking anxiously about as if hoping someone would step in and aid the rancher. But no one was making any move to assist; like John Ashford, all others present were waiting to hear either a denial or a confirmation.

"Come on, four-flusher, you ain't —"

"Go to hell!" Lockwood screamed suddenly in a high, distracted voice, and rocking to one side he snatched Jack King's left-hand pistol from its holster and jammed it into Hungerford's body.

20

The impact of the bullet from the gun Ben Lockwood triggered knocked Cody Hungerford off his saddle, sending him sprawling to the ground amid the churning hoofs of the startled horses.

Instantly everything was in confusion. Jack King spurred about, remaining pistol in hand as he wheeled to face Lockwood. Others in the Hungerford party, caught unawares by the abrupt shift of the situation, were pulling back, all yelling at once.

"King!" Brazil shouted, rushing toward the milling group.

The gunman reversed himself, swung to the lawman. Luke fired as he saw King bring his .45 to quick level. Jack recoiled, buckled, and as the bullet drove into him, began to fall.

Immediately, gunfire erupted among the Hungerford drovers. Bullets spurted dust around Brazil's booted feet, thudded into the wall of the jail behind him, plucked at his sleeve, his hat. He saw Lockwood, still in the center of the melee, sitting high-shouldered in the smoke and haze.

"Ben!" the lawman shouted, "get out of there!"

The rancher seemed not to hear or else was unwilling to heed the warning. As Luke yelled a second time, he saw the rancher stiffen. A bullet fired by one of the drovers had ripped into him. He sagged on his saddle, jolted as another slug struck him.

The street was a bedlam of gunshots and yells. Behind him, on the sidewalk, Brazil heard the boom of a shotgun and realized that John Ashford was taking a hand.

And then, as abruptly as it had begun, it was all over.

The lawman, crouching, drew himself upright, and reloading his pistol, glanced about in the eerie hush. Ben Lockwood was dead. He lay half across the lifeless body of his old enemy, only an arm's length from King, also dead. Two of Hungerford's men were down — one for good, the other sitting flat in the settling dust numbly holding a hand to his side while a stain of blood spread slowly across his middle. Three or four other men, still in the saddle, and a couple who had been standing nearby, showed minor wounds — probably from the shotgun pellets discharged at them by Ashford.

"God in heaven!" Brazil heard him say in a shocked voice.

The lawman glanced at the mayor's stricken face and then threw his glance toward the Antlers as Jenny and her mother, coming off the hotel's porch, were hurrying into the street.

At once, Luke started toward the dead men, hoping to reach Ben Lockwood ahead of them, but both were there before him. He halted a step away, watched as the women crouched briefly beside the cattleman and then rose. The girl's eyes met those of Brazil.

"Jenny — I'm sorry," he murmured.

She stared at him for a long breath, her

thoughts unfathomable, and then, turning to her mother, put her arms around the older woman.

"You wait in the hotel, Mama," she said gently and started for the Antlers. "There're some things I have to take care of."

Brazil shrugged, shifted his hard gaze to the Hungerford riders sitting motionless on their saddles. A fine haze of powder smoke and dust still hovered in the street, now beginning to fill with people.

"I want you all out of town in five minutes."

One of the drovers nodded, pointed to Hungerford and the body of the drover sprawled nearby.

"It all right if we take them along?"

Luke said, "Load them up — King, too — and move out," and beckoned to several local men. "Take Lockwood over to Feeney's. His family will be wanting him there."

"Some of us are hurting bad, Marshal," a drover said, hand on his shoulder. "That damned scattergun —"

Brazil waited until Lockwood had been

lifted from the ground and was being carried toward the undertaker's quarters. The street was crowded now with Moriah residents, all moving in for a look and asking questions.

"The doc's office is on down the street," he said to the complaining trail hand as he pointed in the direction of Middleburg's office. "Get yourself patched up and get out."

"Yes sir," the drover said. Waiting until the bodies of Cody Hungerford and the other dead members of the cattleman's party had been lifted and laid across their saddles, he turned and headed off down the street.

Grim, tension yet holding him wire taut, Brazil pivoted and stepped up onto the sidewalk. Ashford, still clutching his shotgun, was in conversation with Avery Rankin and restaurant owner Pete Spears.

"Obliged to you for backing me up," Luke said to the town's mayor. "Was right when I needed it."

Ashford smiled faintly. "Guns have never been my long suit, but I found out I could use one when it was necessary."

"I was about ready to pitch in —" Spears said and then broke off lamely. "Sure too bad about Lockwood."

"Too bad about the whole damn thing!" Brazil said in a bitter tone, thinking of Arkansas and all the others who had gotten caught up in the problem and were now victims of its backlash. Anger setting his jaw, he faced the crowd. Beyond it, he could see the Lockwood buggy drawn up in front of Feeney's.

"Clear out. Go home or back to your business," he called. "It's all over —"

"Not yet, it ain't," a voice stated flatly from the passageway lying between Rankin's and Schulte's Meat Market.

Motionless, recognizing the voice, Luke rode out a long minute and then came slowly about. Parley Sobel, with a dozen men — some Hungerford's, some his own — drifted quietly into the street in a loose line.

"What I said goes for you, too." Brazil's tone was low, even, carried an insistence.

"Don't mean nothing to me," Sobel said. "Cody didn't get the job done. I aim

251

to do it for him — and me."

"He's dead from trying —"

"Because he was a damn fool showing off! I'm not that way. Me and these boys are going to change this town's mind about closing the trail —"

"And we're starting with you!" the man at Sobel's left shouted. "I owe you special!"

It was Rufe, Garret's friend. Luke nodded coolly, glanced around. With so many persons nearby, a shootout could result in a massacre of innocent bystanders. He should attempt to delay it until the street cleared.

"Been wondering what happened to you," he said to Rufe. And then, "This between you and me or you looking to Sobel and your friends for help?"

Rufe swore, spat angrily. "It's me and you —"

"It's whatever it takes," Sobel cut in. "You shot down one of my drovers —"

"Anybody tell you why? You know what he was doing when I stopped him and Rufe there, and the other one?"

"No, and it don't make a damn," Sobel

said. "I take care of my own. Nobody — not even a tin star — gets away with killing one of my boys! I'm going to —"

"You're doing nothing but moving on," John Ashford said firmly, stepping up to stand beside Brazil. Back of him, Spears, and now Hans Schulte were crowding hurriedly in behind him. Pete had drawn his pistol, was holding it in one hand. Schulte had produced a rifle. "People in this town voted to keep you out. We'll back the marshal all the way."

"We're going to change that vote," Sobel said, "starting right now. I've got a dozen more men ready to take a hand if I need them, so —"

The sudden blast of an explosion across the dead line rocked the settlement, deafening those gathered in the street. As the brilliant flare lit up the sky, revealing bits of soaring wood, rock, earth, and trash, a yell came from somewhere near Dead Ute Creek.

"It's the spur — somebody's blowed up the railroad spur! And the cattle pens are afire!"

21

As one, the crowd began to shift, forming a mass and gravitating toward the crackling fire and slowly settling dust and debris. Shouts could be heard coming from Perdition, where falling sparks and bits of flaming wood were dropping on the roofs of the buildings.

Brazil, facing in the direction of the explosion, had not stirred other than to recoil slightly as the blast shook the town, and the horizon before him abruptly became a blur of dust and shattered wood. His attention was fixed on Parley Sobel and the men siding him, all of whom had glanced wildly over their shoulders at the thunderous interruption and then swung quickly back to face him.

"It's Aaron — Aaron Horn!" someone in the street yelled. "Was him that done it!"

The hurrying crowd parted. Shortly Horn, smoke rising from his clothing in several places, hatless, hair awry, and limping badly, came into view. Drawing abreast of Brazil and the others, he turned sooty, haggard features to them, shook his head.

"That voting weren't enough. I had to fix it good so's they could never come back again," he said in an exhausted voice, and moved on.

A silence fell over the men, and for a long minute there was nothing but the crackle and roar of unchecked flames as the weathered timbers of the cattle pens burned furiously beneath boiling clouds of black smoke. And then, seemingly from far away, yells coming from Perdition could be heard where tinder-dry structures there had caught and were going up.

"I reckon that finishes it," Pete Spears murmured finally, staring at the conflagration. "Ain't nothing left to fight over now."

Parley Sobel shook his head. "It's not over, far as I'm concerned. I've still got to settle with this tin star for killing Len Garret."

"The marshal was doing what we expected of him, keeping the peace," Ashford said. "You want to make an issue of what he was forced to do, take it up with us — the whole town."

Brazil, a hard, half smile on his lips again, the strong pulse of excitement and tension once more throbbing within him, waved Ashford aside.

"Never mind, Mayor — it's me they're wanting to take on," he said and leveled his gaze on Sobel and Rufe. "Is squaring up for Garret worth dying for? That's what it'll cost you, because I'll kill you both."

"Both," Rufe echoed uncertainly, "you figure to take Parley and me both on at the same time?"

Brazil nodded, the fixed smile never leaving his face. "That's how it'll be. Can pick another man to help you if you like — three'll be as easy as two."

Rufe glanced at Sobel. The cattleman in turn was staring at Luke, the shine of sweat on his face.

"There's no need for this, Marshal,"

Ashford protested. "Let the town handle —"

"My problem —" Luke said, shutting the man off, and then to Sobel, added: "Let's get on with it."

It *was* the old days again — a repeat of times past when he'd stood face to face with another man, braced to shoot it out — kill or be killed. It felt good. And why shouldn't it? It was the only satisfying road open to him now. Without Jenny the ranch no longer had meaning, and with Arky dead, gone. . . .

Brazil raised his head slowly, bitter thoughts coming to a stop. Jenny Lockwood was standing in the center of the street staring at him. Her features were strained, worried, and there was an appeal for understanding in her eyes, and hope — and the promise of a future after all if —

The straight, square line of Luke Brazil's shoulders relented. The set, humorless curve of his mouth broke.

"Mayor's right. You want to complain about how I did my job, talk to him," he said, and then added, "Unless —"

Sobel let the word hang briefly,

257

shrugged. "No, I reckon that fellow behind you's right. Town's finished, and so's everything else," he said, and beckoning his drovers with a jerk of his head, wheeled and moved off down the street toward Perdition, now a seething mass of flames and billowing smoke.

"Glad that's over," John Ashford said with a deep sigh. "For a minute there I thought we'd —"

Luke Brazil was paying no attention. His eyes were on Jenny, smiling at him, and waiting there in the smoky haze that was now filling the town. Reaching up, he unpinned the star fastened to his shirt pocket and, handing it to Ashford, hurried to join her.